THE SHARPSHOOTER: REPENTANCE CREEK

TOBIAS COLE

WHEELER PUBLISHING
A part of Gale, a Cengage Company

Smithville Public Library
507 Main Street
Smithville, Texas 78957
512-237-3282 ext 6

GALE
A Cengage Company

Copyright © 2003 by Cameron Judd.
Wheeler Publishing, a part of Gale, a Cengage Company.

LIBRARY OF CONGRESS CIP DATA ON FILE.
CATALOGUING IN PUBLICATION FOR THIS BOOK
IS AVAILABLE FROM THE LIBRARY OF CONGRESS

ISBN-13: 978-1-4328-7073-7 (softcover alk. paper)

Published in 2020 by arrangement with HarperTorch, an imprint of HarperCollins Publishers

Printed in Mexico
Print Number: 01   Print Year: 2020

THE SHARPSHOOTER: REPENTANCE CREEK

1

Five human beings, one of them me, sat inside a lone stagecoach that rumbled in the morning sunlight across the Texas landscape toward the little town of Merritt. Across from me sat a dignified but plainly dressed woman of about sixty, who at the stage depot had been introduced to me as Mrs. Estella Dupont. She was the widow of the Rev. Erastus Dupont, long-time minister of the Merritt Presbyterian Church — a man whose loss, I was informed at the time of introduction, was still much grieved in his home community. Mrs. Dupont was a kindly looking woman who reminded me much of my own mother as she had been at that age. I could not help but notice that the widow seemed preoccupied by the long rifle I'd brought with me onto the coach, the rifle I always carried on my travels, though usually in a case. Not this time, though. The case had been stolen from me about a week earlier while I took target practice out on the Texas plains during a short break in my journey across this vast state. Stolen along with the case was the rifle's scope. Both rifle and scope had been tools of my trade years ago, during the war, when I'd fought as a sharpshooter for Lincoln's army. That grim work had ended for me by my own moral choice even before my capture and subsequent imprisonment at the dreaded prison camp at Andersonville, Georgia. Both the experience of killing other human beings from a distance and that of living like a human swine in the foulest of pens had been for me hells of two distinctive types, but hells indeed, and my life had been forever altered by both of them.

Back during the war, I'd lost the rifle at the time I was taken prisoner, but it was recovered by a friend who managed to return it to me after I came out of Andersonville. It had remained with me ever since, even though — maybe even because — all the memories associated with it were bad ones. It was my duty, I believed, to carry that rifle as a continual self-reminder of what I once had allowed myself to become, and vowed never to let myself become again.

Seated to my right was the man who had

introduced Mrs. Dupont to me: Maximillian Cormondy, gunsmith and merchant of the town of Merritt, and chairman of its town council. Cormondy was one of those friendly types who seemed to know everyone. He'd introduced to me not only Mrs. Dupont, but also my other fellow passengers. This stageline was mostly a local shuttle, and all of the people on it today, other than me, were local people.

Beside Mrs. Dupont was a man in his midtwenties whose name was David Flynn. There was something odd about him, I thought, all centering around the one piece of luggage he carried: a small blue carpetbag, well stuffed, sitting on his lap. The oddity involved not the bag itself, but the intensity with which he protected it. He sat leaning forward, like a selfish dog guarding its food bowl, his chest pressing the carpetbag down onto his lap. Meanwhile, he wrapped his arms around the bag as well, and kept his nervous eyes on the rest of us, orbs flitting from side to side, person to person, as if any one of us might snatch that bag away from him. He paid the most attention to me, the stranger.

Still, I was surprised when he spoke to me. "I think I've met you before, sir," he said.

"Really? When?"

"I don't know . . . but I know I've heard your name. Jed Wells . . . it's familiar. So I must have met you somewhere."

"Not necessarily," I said. "I'm a writer, you see, and you might have seen my name on a book in a library or on a shelf in a shop. Or maybe somebody just said my name and you overheard it."

"Mercy me!" Mrs. Dupont exclaimed. "You surely are not the writer Wells who published those libels against the Confederacy . . . alleging barbarous cruelties and mistreatment in that prison camp . . . are you?"

"I'm the writer Wells who lived through the miseries of Andersonville . . . and who knew many others who did not survive it . . . I'm the writer Wells who wrote as truthfully and forthrightly as he could, through the medium of a novel 'The Dark Stockade,' about what I knew and saw at Andersonville. Then I continued the story of one of the Andersonville survivors in a second novel, 'The Lost Man.' Both books, I'm pleased to say, have enjoyed notable success. And Mrs. Dupont, I assure you that neither book was intended as a 'libel against the Confederacy,' but merely as the most honest tales I could tell."

Mrs. Dupont narrowed her eyes and glared at me, then shifted her gaze toward my rifle again. Her eyes became wet and her lip trembled. Max Cormondy, who had been observing and listening to all this, cleared his throat. "Estella, perhaps you would like me to tell Mr. Wells the reasons for your depth of feeling?"

She nodded.

Cormondy scooted about a little to face me more squarely. "Mr. Wells, I assure you that Mrs. Dupont, the finest of women, meant no slur toward you in what she said. She speaks with a certain passion because the cause of the Confederacy was of great importance to her and her family . . . and because it cost her dearly in the loss of her excellent son, Franklin."

"Mrs. Dupont, I'm truly sorry to hear of the loss of your son," I said. "The war brought such sorrow and loss to far too many good families, on both sides . . . it's an evil thing, war. Even when fought for pure motives and valiant intentions, the evil of it is never fully expunged."

"Truer words never spoken," she said, still looking at the rifle I held.

This time Cormondy addressed Mrs. Dupont. "Estella, I think I can guess what has prompted the tears I see on your face.

11

The rifle Mr. Wells holds?"

"Yes," she said her voice a murmur. "It looks so much like the rifle you gave to Frank when he went off to fight."

"Indeed it does . . . I noticed it myself the moment I saw it. It is very nearly identical." Cormondy went back to talking to me. "Mr. Wells, young Frank Dupont was the finest natural marksman I've ever met, and when he declared his intention to join the Confederate army, I prepared for him a rifle designed specifically for accurate, long-distance, sharpshooter-styled shooting, for I knew he would prove himself in that arena. The rifle I gave him, as you've already heard, looked almost like the one you carry here today. One difference was that I mounted a scope upon Franklin's rifle."

"This rifle also was designed to carry a scope," I said. "But the scope, and the rifle case, were recently stolen. I was a sharpshooter during the war, by the way. I, too, am a naturally skilled marksman."

"A marksman for the side of evil," said Mrs. Dupont. "A killer of fine young men like my own Frank!"

"Young men died on both sides of that war," I said. "All of them had mothers. Even those who you choose to label as being on the 'side of evil.' "

To my surprise, her expression softened and she nodded as if accepting my words. "Yes," she said. "It is mothers who bear the harshest pains of war: the loss of their boys."

"I agree with you, ma'am," I said. "And I hope you will not mind me telling you at this point that your grief is painful to me, because you put me in mind of my own mother when she was your age. She suffered much grief of her own during the war, worrying about my safety, particularly after my capture and imprisonment."

"For her sake, then, as well as yours, I am glad that you made it through the war alive."

"Thank you. And I truly wish your own son had survived. I'm sure he would have been a good man to know."

"He was true-hearted, my Frank. True to what he believed was good and right."

"You could ask for no better from a son than that," I said.

Charlie Crowder shifted in his seat just then and said, "Mr. Wells, if you are indeed a sharpshooter, I'm glad to have you aboard this stagecoach, given what I'm looking at out this window."

"What is it, Charlie?" asked Cormondy.

"Yonder, over where the creek bends through that grove of trees, there's two men, armed and hid amongst the trees. And the one squatted down by the water with that rifle propped up on him . . . is that who I think it is?"

Cormondy craned his neck and looked out the window. "If you think it's Tate Barco, then it's who you think it is."

"Barco!" exclaimed David Flynn, suddenly hugging his carpetbag even closer and looking quite pallid.

"That is indeed Barco," Crowder said. "Which means we have a problem about to present itself to us."

"Maybe not," Cormondy said. "Maybe we'll just roll past and that will be it."

"Yeah, and maybe a rattler won't strike at you if you kick it," Crowder said.

"Who is this Barco?" I asked.

"A terrible man . . . a highwayman and bank robber," replied Mrs. Dupont. "God preserve us!"

"Well, if he's well-known, as I take it he is, then the driver and guard up top will have already noted him and be ready to take evasive action," I suggested.

"I have an idea," Crowder said. "Come over here with that rifle and show us how good a sharpshooter you are by putting a slug through Barco's skullbone."

The words cut through me, knifelike. How could Crowder know that I'd taken a firm

14

vow never again to do the kind of thing he'd just suggested? I wasn't even certain my own arms and hands and eyes would obey me if I tried. My days of treating men as targets were past, and I could not resume them without violating a solemn promise to myself.

"I can't kill a man simply because he sits beside a public roadway," I protested. "We don't know yet whether he intends us any harm. Besides, the guard and driver will protect us from any robbery attempt."

David Flynn said, "If it's Barco out there, there's no question he'll rob us . . . and they won't be able to stop him. He must be prevented from even trying!"

"Right now he's not a stage robber, just a man in a grove of trees," I replied.

"I can see a moral struggle going on inside you, Mr. Wells," Cormondy said. "But let me assure you that killing Barco would not be a murder, but a legitimate act of free American citizens ridding themselves of a blight. The man has already made himself worthy of a bullet in the head by his past crimes. He robbed the bank at Repentance Creek most recently; a bank operated by Albert Flynn, the father of young Mr. Flynn there, and killed a bank guard in cold blood. He's killed others during other robberies as well. We have an opportunity to rid the world of him today, and we must take it."

"If you won't kill him," Crowder said to me, "I will. Just let me borrow that rifle."

"I can't do that . . . I can't be privy to a murder, even indirectly," I said.

"He must be killed," David Flynn declared. "*Must* be killed!"

"I'm no lawyer nor judge, but I think I know enough of the law to say that shooting a man out a stage window, no matter what that man has done in the past, would in the legal sense be murder, and prosecuted as such, especially if that man does nothing but merely sits in a grove of trees at the roadside."

"*Legally* murder, but what about morally, sir? What about all the lives you potentially would be saving by ending his?" Cormondy countered. "By taking Barco's life, you would be saving the lives of others later, no question about it."

"Here's my final word: I can't kill him unless he shows a clear sign he intends to rob or hurt us," I said, trying to remain calm and rational in an atmosphere growing increasingly charged.

David Flynn, still wrapped around his carpetbag, leaned toward me. "Mr. Wells, I cannot tell you how vital it is that Tate Barco be removed. I have a very personal stake in it . . . I am of a banking family and he knows me . . . if he finds me aboard this stage, I truly believe he would take me and demand ransom of my father. He's made such threats before."

Mrs. Dupont said, "When I think of how he so brutally gunned down poor Mr. Jericho at the bank, I feel a great sickness of heart."

"Mr. Jericho was a kind old man who my father paid to help guard the bank . . . it was as much a way of giving an old man a job as it was a serious effort to provide security for the bank," Flynn explained to me. "Barco killed him simply because he tried to do his job and protect the bank. It was pure, unquestionable murder . . . *there's* a new factor for your moral equation, Mr. Wells!"

"I understand your feeling and point of view," I told him. "But the point remains that the law will not see this situation through the same eyes you do. I've never had the ambition to be hanged as a murderer."

At that moment, a rifle fired outside the coach. The coach lurched violently as the horses spooked, and David Flynn, who had been seated on the edge of the bench, flopped onto the floor, still clutching his carpetbag like a child clutching a beloved bedtime toy.

2

"Barco is shooting at us!" Mrs. Dupont wailed.

"No, Estella," said Cormondy. "That was our own stage guard shooting at *him*!"

"Missed him, though," Crowder said at the window. "And now Barco looks riled . . . he's going to shoot back!"

He did shoot back, the crack of his rifle not as loud as the earlier shot from the guard. There was a startling tumult fore and above, something bumping heavily and loudly, tumbling and thumping downward outside and against the coach. Then the coach jumped heavily, once, twice. The guard had just been shot from his perch beside the driver, and had fallen down the outside front corner of the coach and to the ground, where the coach had run him over with both front and rear wheels.

Charlie Crowder thrust his head out the window and looked back along the road behind us to verify all this. When he pulled back in, his face was livid, actually pale despite the deep weathering of his skin. "Anybody eager to defend Barco's right to live now?" he asked, looking at me. "The bastard — sorry, Mrs. Dupont — he committed a murder before our very eyes. Our own guard is lying dead back yonder on the road. Mr. Wells, are you prepared to help us now?"

This time I could not answer as before. The safety and perhaps the lives of all of us depended on it. Barco would shoot the driver next, or the horses, and we would be halted. As witnesses to his murder of the guard, none of us would be safe . . . he might kill us all simply to ensure we did not speak or testify.

I moved over toward Crowder, who left his seat by the window and let me take it. I looked out the window and saw the two men in the trees. "Barco's the taller one, behind the stump," Crowder said. "The other is Hiram Canty, his partner, but him you don't need to worry about so much. He's a coward, and not half the devil Barco is. Just get Barco and Canty will leave us be."

"I'll do my best," I said.

Barco was already taking aim at the stagecoach, targeting the driver. I faced a challenge because of the jolting coach, which now rolled faster than before. It would be quite hard to get off an accurate shot while the coach was in motion, but obviously I could not ask the driver to stop and ensure his own death by making himself an unmoving target.

My odds of actually killing Barco seemed slender, but I reminded myself that I'd managed a similar shot in Virginia once, shooting a Reb officer out of his saddle while I was in the back of a fast-moving wagon on bumpy ground. But I'd been practiced in those days, and had younger eyes, muscles, and nerves then.

I thrust the rifle out the window, pressed the butt of the stock to my shoulder and took aim down the long barrel. Over the bobbing sight I saw Barco, but could draw no bead on him for more than a moment. I steadied myself as best I could and tried to bring my rifle under control.

Barco, who had been aiming at the driver, suddenly turned his rifle in my direction, seeing that I was aiming at him. I figured he could even see part of my face and head inside the shadowed coach interior, and even though I was a moving target, he had the advantage of a firm, unmoving stump upon which to rest his aim. He'd already demonstrated his lethal marksmanship once.

Was I about to pay an ironically appropriate price for all the lives I'd taken during the war? I felt a terrible, odd tingling all over, and a rising of dread.

Something bumped me from behind, generating an outburst of scolding from Charlie Crowder. I glanced over my shoulder. David Flynn was the culprit; he'd come over and was looking over me out the window to see for himself that it really was Tate Barco out there.

"You're spoiling my shot!" I barked at him. He backed away, almost falling over Cormondy's feet.

I resettled. The stagecoach was nearly past the grove and I had to completely shift the angle of my aim. Counting on my training and instincts to guide my timing, I began to squeeze the trigger.

Barco was faster. His rifle fired just as I was jolted once more from behind — Flynn again, trying to balance himself after his near fall. And at that moment, something terrible happened.

I could tell that Barco had aimed at me when he fired, but his shot went high. Flynn made an odd noise and fell backward, landing first in Mrs. Dupont's lap, then rolling onto the coach floor. Barco's bullet had hit him in the lower forehead, passing through his head, shattering the back of his skull. Blood and tissue now stained Mrs. Dupont's dress. She gaped down in horror at Flynn's face, which stared back at her from the coach floor with half-opened unmoving eyes seemingly made of glass.

I aimed quickly at Barco and fired once again, but the distance between us had grown and my shot was hurried and wide. Now I wished I'd listened to the others and acted sooner . . . but how could I have known what was going to happen?

"Dear God above!" Cormondy exclaimed, putting his hand to his mouth as he leaned over and gazed at David Flynn. "Barco's murdered the boy! Murdered him!"

"I told you we should have shot him first thing, Wells!" Crowder said, moving to the front window and drawing his pistol from its holster. He threw three quick and useless shots toward Barco, but was so far off his aim I couldn't even see where the bullets went. Hitting Barco with pistol fire was a hopeless proposition, but I didn't blame Crowder for his effort. At the very least it kept Barco distracted.

But not distracted enough. The outlaw

ducked a little lower behind his stump, aimed again, and fired. I heard a thumping sound above, in the driver's area, and looked at Cormondy as we quietly shared the comprehension that the stage was now moving without a driver. Barco had shot him. Assuming the shot was fatal, there were three dead now: the guard, the driver, and David Flynn.

The driver's corpse remained in its seat instead of tumbling off like the guard had; he'd simply fallen to the side. In fact, I realized, the man might yet be alive. The same thought must have been in Crowder's mind, because he went to the stage door on the side opposite the grove of trees and Barco.

"You can't be thinking of actually trying to get up there," I said. "You'll fall into the wheels!"

"Once I was in St. Louis, and saw a man grinding an organ with a monkey scampering up a brick wall right behind him and dancing on a window ledge," Crowder replied. "I scrambled up right after the monkey. I can climb like one of them California redskins."

"Barco will shoot you!" I protested.

"We're past him now," he pointed out. "He'll not hit me."

But when I looked out the window, I saw

that Barco and his partner Canty were now on horseback, riding after us — and with no driver to urge on the horses, the gap was closing fast. Barco, balancing expertly on his horse, raised his rifle and aimed it at the stagecoach. Dear Lord, the man was about to shoot into the coach itself and let the bullet find whomever it would! I reloaded my rifle, thrust it out the window again, and fired a shot at Barco. It missed, though only narrowly.

He fired right after I did, and something like the blow of a club jolted against the left side of my head and drove me back into the coach, going weak, my rifle falling from fingers suddenly gone numb and clattering to the floor beside me.

I'd just been shot.

Weary now, the horses pulling the coach began to slow. The space between the pursuing outlaws and the stagecoach narrowed even faster. Cormondy pulled a pistol from a holster under his coat and began firing at Barco, and though he was in better range than Crowder had been when he tried a similar tactic, Cormondy was not much of a shot. None of his shots took effect.

Meanwhile, Crowder got the door open, reached to the top of the coach, and found a foothold that let him swing out and up. A lean but muscled man, he made it look easy, though I'm sure the exertion was tremendous.

He gained my admiration when he reached the top of the coach without losing grip. While up there he took two quick shots at our pursuers, but as before, the shots missed. Then I heard him scrambling into the driver's seat . . . and the coach began to slow much more quickly. Crowder had the leads in hand, and apparently had decided it would not be feasible to try to outrun the highwaymen's fresher, less encumbered horses.

Cormondy had emptied his pistol, I had a pistol, but it was above in my luggage, unavailable. And I'd expended all the rifle ammunition I had on my person, the rest of that also stored above. Even if I'd been better situated for ammunition, it wouldn't have mattered. Having just been shot in the side of the head, I was in no shape to fight, anyway.

My head rang like a bell, pain rolling through the entire left side of my skull. I could not see my injury, of course, but Mrs. Dupont, who seemed very little disturbed by the blood, told me a furrow had been plowed across the side of my head, front to back, and that obviously God was with me in that the slightest deviation of angle on the part of the rifleman could have brought me the same sad fate as David Flynn.

I wondered what would become of us . . . much depended upon Barco . . . who had good reason, from a purely practical standpoint, to eliminate us all. We were victims and witnesses of his robbery, and more significantly, witnesses of his murder of David Flynn, the guard, and the driver.

I hoped that Crowder was doing the right thing in stopping the coach. The impulse to keep running was natural, but not logical, given the exhaustion of the stagecoach team, which could not outrun the two riders for long.

The coach halted, and a moment later, Barco was yanking open the door. He trained his rifle on all of us. "Out of there!" he commanded. His partner Canty dismounted and came up behind him. Canty was a stumpy little fellow who carried a shotgun as sawed-off as he was. He waved this about in a very menacing fashion, then in a gravelly voice ordered Charlie Crowder down from the driver's seat, and took Charlie's empty pistol.

"Out!" Barco yelled into the coach, and I moved to obey him. But Max Cormondy was quicker. He spilled out the door while simultaneously pulling out his pistol and relinquishing it to Barco. "A prudent move, sir," Barco said to Cormondy, deftly flipping the pistol in his hand, like a showman, then tucking it into the waist of his trousers. Suddenly Barco shot out his left hand and grabbed Cormondy by the hair, pulling him forward and twisting his head to one side. "Every cent you have, sir . . . in my hat!" Barco let Cormondy go, took off his own hat, and handed it to the gunsmith. Cormondy began emptying pockets, and last of all tossed in his coin purse. Barco nodded and smiled, quite the gentleman now.

Crowder, already disarmed, was robbed next, and I feared everything would blow up right then, because Crowder was uncooperative and defiant. But Barco effectively cleaned him out, though only by having his partner keep that shotgun aimed at all times at Crowder's midsection. Lean as he was, a blast from that shotgun might have blown the man nearly in half.

The widow lost her possessions next, giving them up without resistance, and Barco actually treated her with a degree of deference and courtesy. Then my turn came, and all deference and courtesy vanished. Despite my wounded head and the blood running down onto my shoulder, Barco shoved me about, slamming me against the side of the coach. I suppose he was particularly rough on me because he had surmised by my wound that I was the one who'd aimed a rifle at him out the window. Barco's partner cleaned out my pockets, taking everything from my pocket money to my ivory comb and bone-handled pocketknife. Then we were all lined up together, held at bay by Hiram Canty's shotgun, and Barco went to the open coach door and looked inside at the corpse of David Flynn, which he grabbed by the heels and dragged roughly out. The widow Dupont cried out as if in pain as Barco pulled the body onto the ground. The ruin that was the back of Flynn's head was an ugly, gaping hole, ragged with bone, blood, and brain, and it slammed the ground as Flynn came out and down.

Barco rolled the corpse onto its face with his foot, opened the pocketknife he'd stolen from me, knelt beside the body, and idly poked at the shattered skull tissue with the blade. While he did this horrific act, the point of which utterly escaped me, he smiled up at the rest of us like he was posing for a photograph: the hunter with his kill. It was revolting. Then he rolled the body over again and looked down into Flynn's face with a wicked look of satisfaction. "It's really him, Hiram!" he said to his partner. "This is a prize day, my friend!"

Hiram Canty drifted over and took a light kick at Flynn's body . . . another contemptuous gesture hard to account for. I wondered what lay behind all this strange and hostile behavior. Remembering Flynn's expresssed fear he would be kidnapped by Barco, I recognized that obviously there was a tense history between Flynn and Barco before the stage ever was robbed.

Canty began going through Flynn's pockets, and Barco went back to the door, reached in, and brought out the blue carpetbag. He opened it, looked inside, and grinned. I tried to see the bag's contents, but could not.

"Let's move, Hiram," Barco said, beaming. "We got it back!" He shook the carpetbag.

Canty rose. "What are we going to do with these?" he asked, waving the shotgun at us. "They know us . . . they could talk to the law, or in a courtroom."

"They could, but they won't. These are good, intelligent citizens who know better than to flap their jaws. They care what happens to their kin and their homes and businesses, and they'll not endanger them. Am I right, folks?"

We all quickly agreed, though I, for one, intended to see this pair fully prosecuted and punished for everything they'd done here today. Three murders could not be brushed aside. But at the moment I would act quite agreeable with Barco, because I was the most vulnerable to elimination, not being a local man with kin, home, or business for him to threaten. I had the least to lose by betraying him to the law . . . but if luck was with me, he'd not think of this right away.

3

Barco and Canty put their spoils into every available pocket and into the saddlebags on their horses. Then Barco made a final check of the coach, and came out with my rifle. He also climbed and delved into the storage box under the driver's seat and took out a few things, including some mail. He did not, however, go through the luggage atop the main part of the coach, and thus missed finding my hidden pistol. With his thievery done, he and Canty took all the guns they'd found, including my rifle, mounted up, said farewell to us all as if this were the close of some happy social gathering. With a last warning not to follow or engage the law over this matter, the bandits rode off, ignoring the road and cutting across the plains.

"Well," said Cormondy. "We are all fortunate, at least, to be alive."

"All of us but poor David," said Mrs. Dupont. "Oh, Max, I ache for his family . . .

such tragedies they've suffered, all caused by the same man — robberies, and now the murder of their boy. I know what it is to lose a son . . . I know how deeply this will wound them."

"Yes, yes," said Cormondy. "And speaking of wounds, how are you feeling, Mr. Wells?"

"I've felt better," I admitted.

"You look a sight . . . a wound like that bleeds like the devil, and likely the bullet put a crack in your skull along with that furrow . . . I'll tell you this firmly: don't be thinking of volunteering to join us as we go after Barco and his friend, for you are not up to it."

"So you are going after him?" I asked.

"Indeed. No man threatens my home, business, and kin and simply rides away."

"Nor mine," said Crowder. "Not that I've got a business or a family . . . nor even a home apart from the bunkhouse."

"It's the principle of it that matters," I said. "And that's why, Max, I am going to help out, despite what you just said. He threatened me along with the rest of you, took a rifle that is my most important possession, and even shot me! I have more reason than anyone to want to go after him."

"Is it wise to provoke him?" asked Mrs. Dupont. "He specifically said not to follow,

33

nor to involve the law."

"Are you willing to live with that, Estella, after watching him kill three people?" asked Cormondy.

She thought it over a couple of moments. "No, I'm not. Go after him, Max. Catch him and his little friend, and make them pay!"

"We shall, Estella."

"One question," I said. "Isn't there a sheriff in this county?"

"Yes, and a fine one," Mrs. Dupont said. "He's even famous . . . he was a great Texas Ranger years ago . . . have you heard of Guy Strickland?"

"I can't say I have, ma'am."

"Well, that's our sheriff, and he needs to know about what happened here today."

"And he will, Estella, as soon as we can make contact with him," Cormondy said. "But until then, we can't let Barco and Canty gain too much of a lead. We must pursue now! Charlie and I . . . not you, Jed Wells."

"There are no riding horses, no saddles, and now no weapons," I said.

"There are over there, at Jim Clelland's place," said Charlie Crowder, pointing to the north.

I looked. Less than a mile away was a large

34

house, three stories high, not at all typical of most of the dwellings in this part of the cattle country. The place indicated substantial wealth.

"My thoughts exactly," Cormondy said. "Jim Clelland will give us all we need, and may even ride with us."

"He won't do that," Crowder said. "He's got a busted ankle. Hobbles around on crutches right now. I ran into him at the mercantile at Repentance Creek three days ago, and he was thumping along the boardwalk."

"Well, Mr. Wells can keep him company, then," said Cormondy. "Come on, folks, let's go pay a call on Jim Clelland."

"Get in the coach," said Crowder. "I'll drive us over. But help me get poor Mr. Flynn onto the top, would you, Max?"

Watching that task being carried out was miserable for us all. The horrid wound in the dead man's head leaked fluids and matter, and I said a prayer of gratitude that I hadn't suffered the same kind of fatal head wound. Bad as my wound was, at least I was alive, and would heal and be myself again, healthy and strong. David Flynn was gone forever.

Charlie Crowder was a good coachman, and we reached the ranch house in minutes.

A Mexican foreman greeted Crowder cordially. Crowder braked the coach and lithely descended to the ground. He talked in excellent Spanish to the Mexican man, whose name apparently was Pancho. Though my Spanish was limited, I heard Pancho say that he'd heard at least one of the shots fired in the course of the stage robbery. Once he understood why we were there, he led Charlie Crowder toward the house. Crowder turned and, with motions and mouthed, silent words, indicated that the rest of us should wait, and that he'd return shortly.

I was eyeing the corral, which was filled with excellent horses. If he outfitted the posse with horses like those, they would have a reasonable hope of actually catching up with the highwaymen.

But if I'd been asked to bet on the matter, I'd not have wagered on the posse's success. A local bandit such as Barco would know better than most every secret route, every hiding place, in this region. My guess was that he and Canty were already ensconced at some hidden locale, looking through their take and celebrating a successful robbery.

I left the coach and walked about, forgetting for a few moments about the drying blood that crusted my left shoulder. Then a little Mexican boy, who looked so much like the foreman Pancho that I was sure it must be his son, came around a corner and looked at me in horror, and I was reminded how shocking I surely looked. I smiled at the little fellow, and asked him if he spoke English. He nodded, but backed away, looking very scared. "I need clean water, and a clean cloth, to wash up with," I said. "Do you understand? I was hurt by a bad man, and I need to wash so that I don't look so ugly. And I need a mirror, a looking glass."

The boy nodded again, turned, and ran toward a small, one-story dwelling near the bunkhouse — the foreman's residence, I guessed. I walked around a few minutes more, and the boy appeared again, bearing a basin with water and a cloth draped over the side. He approached me slowly, still scared, so I made sure I did nothing to startle him or make him feel threatened. He held up the basin, which I took, thanking him sincerely. As I carried it toward a nearby stump, the boy followed me, to my surprise.

I sat the basin on the stump, the boy approached, and from a pocket removed a small mirror, which he handed me. I accepted it and thanked him again, then faced a moment of hesitation. I really didn't want to see how I looked, and how bad the wound was.

The boy seemed to sense my thoughts. I was touched as he came near to me, reached out, and gently patted my knee. "You will be well," he said in a high and heavily accented voice. "You will heal."

"Thank you," I said. "I will heal thanks to your kindness and care."

I looked in the mirror and almost wished I hadn't. The furrow was deeper than I'd thought, and the crusted blood on me more abundant. I winced at what I saw in the little looking glass, and the act of wincing made me hurt more, and caused a little fresh bleeding.

I dampened the cloth, which was quite clean and white, and gently wiped at the fresh blood. The dried blood beneath it became liquid again at the touch of the water, and I began to clean it off. Finally the new bleeding stopped, and I began to look a little more human.

The shirt, however, was hopeless. The entire left side was drenched in blood, even down the sleeve. In disgust I rose and stripped the garment off, wadded it up, and tossed it onto the remnants of a burned-out trash fire. I'd buy myself a new shirt at first opportunity, or perhaps some kind person would give me one.

"I'll dump this water out now," I told the boy. "And you be sure that this basin is very well washed before it's used for any reason again, all right?"

"All right," he said.

"What's your name, son?"

"Pablo," he said, beaming at me, obviously proud of his name.

"Pablo, you are an excellent young man. Is your father the foreman here?"

"Yes . . . he is in the house now, with Senor Crowder."

"You know Charlie Crowder, obviously."

"Yes . . . he once worked here, with my father. My father, he thinks Senor Crowder is a very good man."

"I don't really know him, but I have a good impression of him as well."

"He can do anything, my father tells me. He is strong and smart and a good cattleman . . . but not as good as my father, of course."

"Of course."

I dumped the water, which now had a pinkish tinge, and shook the last drops out of the basin. Then I wrung out the cloth and tossed it onto the old burn pile, atop my discarded shirt. Pablo took the basin and mirror and carried them back to his house.

At the ranch house, the door opened and Charlie Crowder emerged, followed by a stranger with silver hair, the face of a man in his sixties, and the form of a man of thirty. Muscled and limping, he was almost as lean as Crowder. This, I assumed, was Clelland, owner of this massive spread.

Cormondy joined them, shaking hands with Clelland. Clelland looked around at our group, bowing respectfully toward Mrs. Dupont, then staring at me, the stranger with the wounded head and no shirt. He stepped down from the porch and strode toward me. We shook hands and made introductions.

"You got that wound in the robbery, did you?"

"Yes, sir. Barco fired into the coach and I took the slug across the side of my head. I could use a bandage if you might have some cloth to spare."

"We'll get you taken good care of. But first I've got to outfit these other men with some horses and guns . . . though I have doubts about their prospects for success. I know Barco . . . hell, the man once worked for me, back before he turned crooked . . . and he'll find a hole to hide in that they'll never

uncover. But I don't blame them for looking."

"I want to go with them."

"Don't think you should, sir. A head
wound like that can cause you problems
when you ain't looking for them. You could
pass out, lose your vision, get sick to your
stomach . . . any number of things."

"I suppose you're right."

"Have a seat on the porch there, and I'll
have you in good hands before you know
it."

The porch held three huge oaken rocking
chairs. I settled myself into the one closest
to the door and relaxed as I watched Cormondy and Crowder head for the corral.
After a few moments in the comfortable
chair, with a breeze coming around the
corner of the house, I closed my eyes. When
I opened them again the sun was an a different part of the sky, and a broad, very dark
woman with coal-black hair piled atop her
large head stood in front of me, hands on
hips, somewhat harsh gaze fixed on my face.
"I thought you were dead for a moment,"
she said. "You breathe very shallow breaths,
senor."

"I'm sorry." Looking at her more closely,
I realized that she, too, bore a resemblance
to young Pablo. So I smiled at her and said,

41

"Ma'am, your son is a good boy . . . I hope you are quite proud of him."

"Quite proud, senor. Thank you." Then she aimed a finger at my nose. "But I tell you this, senor, kind words from you or no, I will hold you and all your companions from the stagecoach accountable if my husband suffers harm."

"Your husband went with the posse?"

"He did . . . and I fear for him, senor."

"I'm . . . sorry. I wish he'd not gone."

"So do I, sir. Was it him who was robbed and shot on the stagecoach? No! But is it him who is out searching for the bad men who would kill him and care nothing for it? Si! And yet you sit sleeping on this porch, you who were robbed and shot, but who are content to let other men do your duty."

"Ma'am, I was not allowed to go. I wanted to do it! But my wound . . . they told me I was not fit for it."

"This Barco is an evil man . . . and he hates Mexican people, I have heard. If there is trouble, it will be my husband who finds it. Barco will not let a Mexican man who goes against him escape unpunished."

"I'm sorry to hear this. But things may work out better than you believe. The most likely event is that they will not find the bandits at all."

"I hope they do not. Now, come inside . . . I will bandage your wound, so the flies will leave you in peace."

"Thank you . . ." I'd not thought about flies until she said that. All at once I really wanted that bandage. I got up, too fast, and was hit by a jolt of vague dizziness.

"Senor, are you going to fall?" she asked, reaching for me.

"No, no . . . I'm fine. I just don't get a bullet through the skull every day."

"Inside, Senor Wells."

"Thank you, Senora —"

"Call me Rosalita, sir."

"Fine . . . if you'll call me Jed."

Within minutes, a crisp, sparkling white cloth surrounded my wounded noggin, expertly wrapped and tied. Before putting it in place, Rosalita had dressed the injury with some sort of homemade ointment, which felt remarkably soothing.

Clelland was still present, which surprised me. I'd figured he'd have joined the posse . . . he just looked like the kind who would.

From another adjoining room, this one on the opposite side from Clelland's den, a low, rumbling noise drifted out. Snoring . . . then a woman's voice, murmuring as if in sleep.

I recognized the voice: Mrs. Dupont. In there napping and snoring.

Clelland had a brandy in hand when he entered the room from his private den and office adjoining, and when he saw me awake and being treated by Rosalita, vanished into his private area again and emerged a second time, now with two brandies. He offered me one, which I gladly accepted even though it was early in the day for drinking. This was not a normal day.

"Rosalita's got you wrapped up good, Mr. Wells," he said.

"Yes, sir. She's a good nurse."

"Good nurse, good housekeeper . . . good at midwifing a calf in a troubled birth, too. The woman can do anything. Just like her husband. Good folks, that family."

"She told me her husband has gone off with the manhunters."

"Yep, he did it. I advised him not to, but he was determined. And you can't talk that stubborn old Mex out of nothing if he sets his mind on it."

"I should have gone, not him," I said, sipping my brandy.

"With a wound like you got, I don't know about that. Though I admit that you don't look nearly so bad off now that Rosalita has done her wrapping job on you."

44

"Then give me a horse and a rifle, just on loan, of course, and let me go after them."

His answer surprised me. "You think you're up to it?"

"I do," I said.

"Then come on. We'll get you ready to go. I'm glad you're going . . . I have a notion they might need a man with shooting skills, and I'm told you were a sharpshooter."

We carried our brandy with us and headed out to the corral.

"You coming too?" I asked Clelland.

"No . . . too old for such, at least while there's younger bucks around to do it in my place. I had my time at such work myself, once, back when I was in the Rangers."

"Somebody told me the sheriff here was a Ranger, too."

"Yeah, he was. Guy Strickland was one of the greats. Can't say I was. I couldn't hold a candle to light that man's cigar. But I did my best, and got my fill of manhunting and such. So I'm content to let the younger bucks do it now."

"I'm no young buck, but I do want to bring in Barco," I said. "The man's a murderer of the worst variety."

"You'll get no argument from me on that."

We reached the corral, and I began looking over the horses. "Pick one out," he said.

"They're all good ones — especially that black with the star over yonder. You pick your horse and I'll go back in the house and open the rifle case."

"I'll join you in a few minutes," I said.

He walked back to the house, and I turned my attention to the horse with the star on its muzzle.

4

The sun was brighter, the day growing hotter, but my borrowed horse was strong and fast of pace. I rode now on the road toward Repentance Creek, the same road taken by Barco and Canty, and by the band of manhunters after them. So far, I'd caught up with no one, and was not certain that either group had stayed long on this road.

Ahead, though, something of interest had come into view. Two riders, leading what initially appeared to be a packhorse, were heading in my direction. One was a burly, rugged fellow who might be a cattleman, the other a much smaller man who was busy with his hands as he rode, scribbling with a pencil on a small pad of paper.

My interest in the pair heightened dramatically when they came close enough for me to note two things: the bigger man had a star-shaped badge gleaming on his vest, and the "pack" on the back of the third horse

47

was not a pack at all, but a human body, draped face-down over the saddle and tied in place. It was the body of a rather short, thick fellow, and my heart leaped toward my throat as I recognized in profile the familiar person of Hiram Canty. I pulled my horse to a halt and sat gaping as the riders came up to me.

I looked at the man with the badge. "Sheriff Guy Strickland?" I asked.

"That's me, friend. And this here is Pembrook Jones, the editor of the RABUN COUNTY ADVOCATE, our local newspaper. And the man on the horse is one Hiram Canty, a local no-good and highwayman who fled this vale of tears a little earlier with the help of someone who obviously was not much happy with him."

"I recognized him. That man robbed the Merritt-bound stagecoach this morning, along with another man whose name was given to me as Tate Barco. The coach is sitting back at the Clelland Ranch yonder way, if you want to examine it. This horse and rifle is on loan to me by Mr. Clelland. And my name is Jed Wells . . . I'm a newcomer here."

"Well, I'm sorry your welcome to our county involved stagecoach robbery," the sheriff said. "Not the kind of impression we wish to make, no sir."

"I fault only the robbers, not the county, sir. Do you know who killed Canty?"

"Not for sure. I think it might have been his own partner. The two were known to squabble."

"There was a posse of manhunters — two of them others who were on the robbed stagecoach — who went after the highwaymen. Perhaps they found them."

"No . . . I know the group you mean — Max Cormondy and Charlie Crowder, and that Mexican foreman of Clelland's . . . I passed them earlier and they hadn't found nobody, and by then Canty was already dead."

"You should know, sheriff, that there was more than stagecoach robbery that took place. There was murder as well. Barco shot into the stage more than once, wounding me with the first shot, and killing a young man named David Flynn with another."

"So I was told by Max. Terrible, just terrible. The Flynns are good people, even if Albert has a bit of conceit about him, and even though father and son were so shamefully and unfortunately estranged. Now there's no opportunity for them to reconcile."

"It is too bad if they were estranged," I

said. "That does make a sad situation even sadder. Sheriff, if you need to officially identify the body, it is on the coach at the Clelland house, unless someone has moved it since I left."

"I do need to identify it. But Max said others were killed, too."

The newspaperman was writing as fast as he could, trying hard to catch every new turn of this conversation.

"Yes," I said. "The guard and the driver were both killed, also by Barco. Had he been only a slightly better shot, I would be among the dead as well."

"I'm glad you are not. Maybe now we'll finally get an opportunity to make that varmint swing like he deserves," said Strickland. "Where are the other two bodies?"

"The driver remained in his seat when he died and I assume is still there. The guard fell off and was run over by the coach. I suppose he must still be lying on the road."

"This is all so unbelievable," said Jones, still scribbling.

"I assure you, it's all true," I replied. Then I asked the sheriff: "Do you know where Max and the others went? I'd like to catch up to them if it is possible."

"They were just this side of Repentance Creek when Pembrook and I saw them."

"I'm curious, sir: were you called out because of the stagecoach robbery?" I asked.

"No, no, nothing that substantive. What drew me out was just a worthless husband spatting with his wife. She'd taken a rolling pin to him — and he deserved it, the way he'd slapped her about — but after she struck him he decided he'd take an oak pole to her. She didn't deserve that, and he's a good 240 pounds, maybe more. The neighbors saw the battle and sent a boy into town to find me, and he came in just at the time Mr. Jones here was sitting down to talk to me for his newspaper. He seems to find me of interest because of my history with the Texas Rangers."

"And I'm sure that is an interesting history, Sheriff."

"Be that as it may, by being in my office when he was, Mr. Jones found himself with the opportunity to accompany me in answering a citizen's call. He came to the scene with me, and watched me deal with it. Now, I know many believe a man has a right to beat his wife, but I don't accept that at all. The Good Book says to treat your wife as a part of yourself and love her as Christ loves the church. That's my own viewpoint as well. So I settled that marital battle down right quick, though Bailey

Freeman — that's the husband who was doing the beating — didn't take to it very well, and threatened to backshoot me when he got the chance."

"I think he meant it, too," said the newspaperman. "He sounded serious."

"This Freeman . . . has he got a thick shock of red hair, and a big belly?" I asked.

"He does indeed," the sheriff replied. "But how do you know that?"

"I don't . . . but there's a man over in those woods, watching us from behind a fence, who matches that description . . . and he's got a rifle."

"Good Lord!" Jones yelped, ducking down almost flat in his saddle as only a man as small as he could do. The sheriff didn't react so extremely, but he did turn and look with an expression of concern in the direction I was facing.

"Yep, that's him," he said, spotting the man I'd referenced. "That's Bailey Freeman. I guess he figured to get his backshooting done sooner rather than later."

"Sheriff, you must move to cover . . . look — he just raised that rifle . . . he's got it resting on a fencepost and aimed your way!"

The sheriff, brave man though I'm sure he was, was also a smart and prudent one. He quickly put his horse in motion, heading toward a ravine that ran parallel to the road, about 20 yards away. He rode down into the ravine just as Freeman fired his shot. The slug zipped past me and in the general direction of the sheriff, but missed. The newspaperman made a whimpering noise, then followed the sheriff's course into the ravine, leaving me alone on the open roadway.

I knew my duty. I raised the rifle I'd obtained from Clelland, and for the second time in one day violated my long-standing vow to put aside my wartime sharpshooting ways. I took careful aim at Freeman, and he took note of it and swung the rifle toward me. Even from this distance I could see the black eye of the muzzle opening. Before he could fire, I fired, and his body bucked and fell backward. I watched him writhe a moment, then grow still.

The sheriff, drawn back out by the gunfire, came out of the ravine, Jones following and scribbling with amazing speed. Strickland came to my side. "You got him?"

"I did. It was self-defense, sheriff. He'd taken aim at me at the time I fired."

"You need not worry about legal repercussions from this," he said. "The man tried to kill an elected officer of the law. And he would have done so if not for your warning."

"You are a *hero,* Mr. Wells," said Jones, writing now with grand flourishes of the hand. "Heroically defending both the guardians of the law and the rights of downtrodden women!"

"I'm no hero . . . just a man who tries to do the right thing, when the right thing is clear. Most of the time, for me, it isn't so clear . . . or maybe I just am stricken with occasional moral blindness."

"I'm not trying to annoy by writing these things down, sir . . . simply to do my job as a journalist. To work as a journalist is to make a silent promise to the public to give them the news they deserve . . . and I must fulfill that promise."

"Might as well take Pembrook at his word, Mr. Wells," said Strickland. "I learned long ago that Pembrook Jones here is as stubborn as he is runty — sorry, Pembrook. He'll do what he wants no matter what you say. But at least he does what he does out of a sense of duty. If he got the notion that the public had a moral right to see the bare backside of the governor, he'd be hauling a camera or a sketch artist off to the capitol latrine right now."

"Like you, Mr. Wells, I try to do the right

54

thing as I am able to perceive it," Jones said, basking boyishly in the sheriff's colorfully worded praise.

"Fine . . . but please, if you will, don't dwell on me as a 'hero' because I shot somebody. That touches nerves in me that you cannot be aware of."

"The public will decide the question of heroism, sir. All I can do is present the facts so that they may do so."

I could see that Strickland was right: no use arguing with this fellow. I'd just hope for the best when his report came out. I'd had my troubles with newspapers before; I remembered the difficulties a newspaper had given me in Kansas, when I was helping out an old friend who was a town marshal there. I'd survived that time, and I'd survive whatever Jones might dish out.

He paused beside the dead man and began examining him and writing at the same time. A description of the corpse, I suppose. It seemed foolish to me. I'd seen enough dead men to know that death was death, and there was little about it worth looking at, much less describing.

The sheriff looked toward Repentance Creek, the squatty skyline of which was outlined against the Texas sky. "Mr. Wells, you might be interested in what's coming down the road toward us."

I turned and saw riders — then recognized the slender form of Charlie Crowder on the lead horse. The manhunters, with no one extra in tow, were coming back the way they'd gone.

"By the way," I asked the sheriff, "how does a town get a name like Repentance Creek?"

"You ever heard of that camp meeting preacher name of Edward Killian?"

"Yes, indeed. I knew the man briefly, in Kansas."

"He had one of his first big camp meetings along the banks of the creek that runs through town. Very successful, I'm told, folks flocking in, getting converted, repenting right and left. Hence the name of the creek, and then the name of the little town that grew up along it."

"Makes sense."

"Yep." Strickland raised his hand and waved. "Howdy, Max Cormondy! Howdy Charlie Crowder! Howdy there, Pancho Valdez!"

The trio greeted the sheriff cordially but solemnly. Then the corpse of Hiram Canty preoccupied them. Charlie Crowder rode over a little closer to it and gave Canty a soft kick on the back of the head. Nobody objected to the rudeness. I remembered Canty's own abuse of David Flynn's body, and the old cliche about what goes around comes around came to mind.

"At least one of them's gone," he said.

"Gentlemen, on a day such as this one, I wish very hard that I'd been more success-ful in my response to the Repentance Creek bank robbery," said Sheriff Strickland. "Had I been able to catch Barco after that rob-bery, he'd be locked up right now, facing murder charges for the death of Mr. Jer-icho, and David Flynn and the stagecoach driver and guard would be alive right now."

"You do what you can with little to no help, sheriff," said Cormondy. "This county gives you almost no support in your func-tion . . . not even enough money to hire a deputy!"

"I appreciate your comprehension of my situation, Max . . . but I'll not lay off my own failures on external circumstances. I should have tried harder to get Barco. If I had, maybe none of this would have hap-pened today."

"I'll be sure and make reference in my story to the lack of funding provided to your office, Sheriff," said Jones, scratching on his notepad again.

"Who knows, Pembrook? Maybe it will

help. Did you men see any sign of Barco, Max?"

"No . . . none. But who is this man?" He pointed at the would-be assassin on the ground.

"A man who tried to kill me, and who was summarily dealt with by Mr. Wells here," Strickland said.

Max looked closely at the dead man. "Is that Bailey Freeman?"

"It is."

"Huh! Well, I'm not surprised he's come to a bad end. The man had little to recommend him, and he was quite cruel to his family."

"Maybe so," I said. "But I take no joy in having had to kill him."

"I wish your shot at Barco had been as true as this one," said Cormondy.

"So do I," I replied.

Crowder spoke: "Max, you misspoke when you said we found no sign of Barco. Show what's in your saddlebag."

Cormondy opened a saddleback and from it pulled the blue carpetbag that David Flynn had guarded. "This was on the ground at that old barn just this side of town," he said. "I guess Barco rode through that way."

"He did . . . and it was near there that I

58

found the body of our friend Hiram Canty," said Strickland.

"David Flynn guarded that bag like it held the crown jewels of every nation," I said. "What's in it now?"

"Nothing," said Cormondy. "Except a few empty banknote wrappers from the Repentance Creek Bank . . . and this was in there, too." From a pocket he produced a small metal hinged box, quite flat. I took it and examined it, flipped back the latch, and opened it.

It wasn't really a box, but a picture frame with a folding lid, functioning like an oversized locket. Inside was a photographic portrait of a young woman, about twenty, I suppose, dressed in a high-collared, formal-looking dress, her back straight as a board as she posed for the camera. She was quite pretty, her eyes in particular being striking and intense.

"Who is she?" I asked, showing the portrait all around.

"I don't know her," Cormondy said, "so I suspect she is not a local girl."

"I've seen her," said the sheriff. "I don't know where, though, nor who she is."

"She must have been a friend or lover of David Flynn," I said. "Why else would he have her picture?"

"Tell you what," threw in Crowder. "I'd carry about a picture that pretty if for no other reason than to look at it. But you're right . . . most likely she was Flynn's gal."

"His family will know her, then," I said.

"I suppose so," said the sheriff. "But what does it matter? Whoever she is, she's got no more involvement in this matter than having her picture turn up in an empty carpetbag."

"Yes . . . but a carpetbag obviously filled before with bank money," I said. "Why would David Flynn carry a bag of money from the Repentance Creek bank on a stagecoach?"

"His father owns the bank," said Crowder. "I'd say it's easy for him to get at the money."

"But why? Why carry it around?"

"Good question indeed," Strickland said.

"Wait a minute," Crowder said. "Wait just a minute . . . do you remember, Jed, when Canty was digging into the carpetbag during the robbery, and he said to Barco that they should go ahead and leave because they 'got it back'?"

"Yeah, I heard him say that, too. 'Got it back.' And he was looking in the bag when he said it. Looking at the money, obviously."

"So he was telling Barco they'd got the

money back."

"Which implies they'd had it before, and lost it," I said. "So the money in that bag must have been at least some of the money they'd robbed from the bank."

"But how did David Flynn get his hands on it?" Crowder asked.

"I don't know, and unfortunately, we can't ask him."

"Let me talk to you a minute, Jed," said Crowder. He moved his horse over a few yards, away from the rest, and looked over his shoulder and indicated with a jerk of his head that I should follow.

I did, curious about this secrecy. Crowder pulled a small cigar from his pocket and lit it while I approached. Puffing smoke, he looked at me through the cloud, and said, "Got something I want to ask you about. Are you a man who follows his impressions, his instincts?"

"Most of the time."

"Well, sir, I am too, and my instinct tells me that Max Cormondy is a lot better gunsmith than he is a manhunter. If we'd pressed on after finding that carpetbag, and followed the tracks that were there, and talked to some of the people who live about there and may have seen something . . . we'd have found Barco. I believe it, anyway."

"So you're saying?"

"That maybe the key to all this is that pretty gal in the picture. David wasn't carrying that for no reason. And odds are good that she's someone who somebody around here knows. I can think of one person worth asking."

At that moment, so could I. "Mrs. Dupont?"

"Exactly. She knows more people around here even than Cormondy does. I got a proposition for you: let's get the good sheriff over there to deputize us. Then let's you and me go visit the widow Dupont, and look on our own for Barco. I believe we can find him. I don't think Max will. And if we can find that girl, too, maybe we'll learn how David came to have that money in his possession."

Whatever it was, I found myself agreeing to Crowder's proposition. Deputies we'd be, if the sheriff would have us. When we rode back to the others, Cormondy announced that the posse was disbanded, the matter now back fully in the hands of the sherriff, to handle as he saw fit. The sheriff didn't look very happy, but I noticed he didn't push to keep Cormondy's posse together, either.

After some friendly words of parting, Cor-

mondy turned his horse and rode with Pancho back in the direction of the Clelland
Ranch.

ficed, turned his horse and rode with I'm-
the back in the direction of the Cashand
Ranch.

5

Crowder and I went to the sheriff. Charlie said, "Sheriff, I'd like to ask you to swear in me and Jed here as temporary deputies. We want to keep looking for Barco, and it would be good to have some official standing as we do that."

"Why, Charlie, you ain't got a lick of experience in law tending, have you?"

"No, sir."

"I do," I said. "I was a town deputy in Kansas for a time, helping out an old friend of mine who was marshal."

"Good enough," he said. "Stick your right hands in the air and say, 'I accept the post of deputy and will in that capacity uphold and defend all laws of Rabun County and the state of Texas, and will answer to the direction and supervision of the Rabun County Sheriff.' "

We mumbled out the lines, and Crowder said, "You just made that up right then, didn't you!"

"Maybe I did, boys. But it will do the job. Now, what's our plan?"

"First of all, we're going to follow Max and Pancho back to the ranch and talk to the widow of the late Rev. Dupont from Merritt. You remember him? Well, his widow knows the Flynn family well, and might know that girl in the picture. We have a feeling the girl, if we can find her, might know some things about how David Flynn came to have stolen bank money in his bag."

"How do you know it was stolen?"

I explained my reasoning as best I could. Strickland seemed to follow and accept it.

We rode back, catching up with those who had already gone ahead. Mrs. Dupont was still at the ranch, seated in one of the front porch rockers as we rode in. With Clelland standing by, she looked at the portrait of the girl, frowning in concentration. "I've seen that young woman," Clelland said. "In Repentance Creek, I think. Yes . . . that's right. I remember. Somewhere in Repentance Creek."

"Do you know her name?" Crowder asked.

"Her name is Mary, I think," Mrs. Dupont said. "David Flynn told me that."

"Flynn?"

65

"Yes. Poor David was quite smitten by her, and talked about her with me quite a bit."

"What is her last name?"

"I don't know. He never told me, close friends as we were. He declined to talk about her family, which I always thought odd since he had come to view me as his substitute mother, in a way. His real mother died when he was only ten years old. Such a tragedy! But not as great as the tragedy of his relationship with his father."

"What do you mean by that?" I asked.

"The two of them fell away from one another a year or two ago. A lot of little reasons, the typical things that cause fathers and sons to argue — conflicting plans and visions, different views of the world, a father's ambitions for a son not matching those of the son himself. And I think maybe this girl as well . . . Albert didn't like her for some reason. David and his father allowed such things to push them far apart, and they never reconciled. I dread the sorrow that Albert Flynn will suffer when he learns that his final chance to make peace with his son is gone."

I told her about the money wrappers in the carpetbag and asked if she had any idea why David would have been carrying bank money to Repentance Creek. She seemed troubled by the question.

"I don't know."

I mentioned that cryptic comment from Canty about "getting back" the money, and she said she'd heard it, too. That comment more than any other thing cast an air of mystery around this whole affair. And as a writer constantly looking for new ideas that could develop into stories, a mystery was something hard to let go of.

Clelland's houseful of unintended guests was soon significantly depeleted. The stagecoach had been retrieved by the stageline while we were out on our manhunt, so the rancher outfitted a big wagon with temporary bench seats, threw a canvas cover over the whole thing, and created a makeshift stagecoach, upon which Mrs. Dupont and Max Cormondy resumed their journey to Merritt. Pancho served as driver. Crowder and I, with our newly sworn duties as deputies, remained at the ranch, which would serve as our base from which to seek Barco.

Mrs. Dupont left the ranch with a heavy heart, having taken on by her own volition the responsibility of confirming to David Flynn's father that his son was dead. By now, the news of the robbery and deaths was bound to be out in the form of rumor at the very least, but official confirmation had probably not yet become public. I admired Mrs. Dupont for being willing to take upon herself such a sad duty.

Crowder and I spent the last hours of daylight covering the ground that had been covered earlier. We sought I don't know for what . . . mostly we were following another "impression" of Crowder's — a feeling he had that Barco would return to the crime area, where we'd be able to take him into custody. I, for one, thought it unlikely.

It was an odd thing for me, serving as an official, even if unpaid, representative of the law of a county and state in which I was a stranger. Why was I doing it? Crowder asked me, and I'd already asked myself.

The only answer I could come up with was summarized in a single word: duty. I owed it to myself to see Barco brought to justice, and to those who had died . . . especially the one who had died taking a bullet originally intended for me.

"Mr. Wells, tell me about your writing, and how you spend your life," Clelland asked me as we sipped coffee and ate supper after Crowder and I finally returned from the latest search of the robbery scene.

I told the rancher of my war experience,

the miseries of my life as a sharpshooter, the ordeal of capture, and the realization of what had befallen me the day I strode through the gate of a tall, dark stockade, and heard myself called a "fresh fish" by the men who had already grown accustomed to the horrors of Andersonville. I entered Andersonville a "fresh fish" and left little changed . . . I never did grow accustomed to the place, to the horror, as some had been able to do, to a degree. But over time in captivity I discovered I possessed two valuable gifts. One was the gift of words — the ability to tell stories in a compelling and moving way — the other the companion gift of truly listening, truly hearing and grasping deeply the stories that others told me. I found others in that terrible prison were drawn to me for reasons not clear to me, but which I believe had to do with those gifts. They told me about their lives, homes, families . . . and some of the least fortunate prisoners, those who knew they were never going to leave that dreadful prison, gave to me messages for loved ones at homes scattered across the country. These messages they asked me to carry to their families after I was free, and I promised dozens of them to do that very thing.

Ultimately, it was the writing that empowered me to fulfill those promises — an activity still in progress for me. For a long while after I put Andersonville behind me, I left the task undone because I had neither the time nor the resources to complete it. Then came my first book, and with it unexpected success. The memory of those promises made to dying men in a prison camp returned to me, and I began to fulfill them. And that quest, which took me across the country, ever on the move, ever meeting new people, was now the strongest driving force of my life, the thing that gave me purpose and meaning, the reason, I believed, that I had been put in the world and through the rigors I'd experienced. I told all of this to Clelland, sensing that he held an authentic interest in it.

"I'm impressed by your calling, and your attitude toward fulfilling it," Clelland said. "I can think of little more valuable and meaningful than delivering such important and personal messages to those who otherwise could never receive them."

"It's my duty to the living, and to the dead," I said. "I take satisfaction in carrying it out."

"Tell me this: have you ever considered simply publishing those messages in a book, saving yourself the trouble of having to find

70

so many individuals and famiies . . . which cannot be an easy task?"

"No, it isn't easy . . . but a book is too public a forum. I could not write these messages into a book without violating the personal and private nature of them. Some things can only be told to those intended to hear them, and to no others."

"A good answer, sir, showing you are a man of the proper prudent and moral sensibilities. An important gift for a writer, I believe."

"You flatter me, sir," I said.

"I am eager to read your work, Mr. Wells," Clelland said. "I intend to make a visit to the local library and obtain a copy of 'The Dark Stockade.' I believe I'll better enjoy such a work having met you in person and," his voice dropped to a whisper, and he exclaimed, ". . . my *God!*"

Clelland had the oddest of expressions on his face all at once.

"What is it, Jim?" asked Crowder.

"I just remembered something, as we talked about the library. I've seen that girl in the portrait . . . *at the library.*"

"Are you certain?" I said.

"Quite certain. I don't know why I didn't remember that before. But I know I saw her there, working behind the desk with Mrs.

71

Stover, the librarian. I noticed her because of her beauty."

"I think we'll be making a visit to the library ourselves, then," Crowder said. "Maybe we'll find the girl."

A huge chocolate cake was Rosalita's final contribution to supper. It was served in the sitting room and devoured with the intense appreciation it deserved. When the final plates were put away for washing, a knock on the door heralded a visit from Sheriff Strickland, who had come by to see if his new volunteer deputies had enjoyed any luck in finding Barco.

Strickland himself had not. He'd covered ground again and again, asked questions of potential witnesses, and toured places where Barco was known to hide out, all to no avail. When Strickland asked us about *our* progress, Crowder looked at me in a way that told me I was the designated spokesman.

I decided to say nothing about what Clelland had just said about the girl in the portrait, and the library, because we had no inkling yet as to whether this would prove a substantive matter or a blind alley.

"We're no closer to Barco than we were," I told Strickland. "No news, no evidence regarding him."

"I release you from your commission as

deputies, then, if you wish that. It should not be your burden to do the task I am paid to do."

"Sheriff, I for one would like to retain that commission," I said. "I watched a young man die with a bullet in him that was fired at me . . . fired by a man I had failed to kill when I had the chance. And that same man stole from me a rifle that was given me by my late father, and which went with me through one of the hardest periods of my life. Wanting to see Barco brought to justice is personal for me now . . . but should I encounter him, it would be helpful to hold a legal standing to bring him in . . . or bring him down, as the case may be."

"Any citizen can bring in a wanted criminal, not just a law officer," said Strickland.

"Yes . . . but a man has a greater sense of authority in his own mind if he has an official standing."

"Well, I wouldn't matter to Barco either way. He holds no respect for the law at all, and he'll kill anybody who tries to interfere with him whether or not he holds a rank or is just a citizen."

"Have a piece of this cake, sheriff?" asked Clelland.

"No thanks, Jim, I done ate my supper and had a big old slab of apple pie with cream on it. I couldn't eat another bite . . . though I know how good a cake Rosalita makes."

Strickland didn't linger long, and with supper and a long, trying day now behind, I could think of nothing but sleep. But I did lend a hand to Rosalita, over Clelland's protest in that I was his guest, and helped her wash dishes, an act of unselfishness that obviously elevated me to something near sainthood in Rosalita's eyes. This hard-working woman obviously was not accustomed to much voluntary help.

After the dishes were washed, I went back to the main sitting room, where I sank into a comfortable chair and picked up an old copy of the RABUN COUNTY ADVO-CATE. Flipping through it, I found stories by Pembrook Jones. Not a bad writer, this fellow . . . his sentences were sharp, clear, and terse, his paragraphs of restrained length — unlike so much journalism of the period — and packed with information. I'd seen far worse on the front pages of major newspapers.

I wondered when Jones would publish his story based on the day's events — soon, I supposed . . . the next edition, surely, while the news was fresh. I was under no illusion that my part in the stagecoach incident, and my shooting of Bailey Freeman, would escape coverage, as much as I would have liked to do so — especially the latter part. But Jones had witnessed me killing Bailey, the would-be assassin, and was obliged to write about it. But I dreaded it. That kind of publicity I did not need, even if Jones portrayed me as a heroic savior of a popular sheriff and scourge upon cruel wife-beaters, as I anticipated he would do, based on his behavior and attitude at the scene of the incident.

I asked Clelland about the publication schedule of the newspaper; he told me the next edition would print the next afternoon. So if Jones had been a busy fellow through this afternoon and evening, his reporting on the day's events would be in the news by this time the next day.

Clelland said, "I ain't prone to pry into a man's private affairs, Jed, so I hope you don't mind this question. I'm just curious if you've come to Texas on one of your ventures to talk to somebody about the prison camp, as is your habit."

"Not this time," I told him. "I'm here to meet a rancher, in fact, a man named Walter Gage."

"Oh, I know Walter well. His spread is part in this county, part in the next. A good man, but a tenderfoot cattleman. He don't know a heifer's hind foot from a bull scrotum, just to say it straight out. How do you know Walter, not being from here?"

"Well, if he's a tenderfoot in ranching, he's a veteran in the publishing business. Walter Gage founded the publishing house that publishes my books. Further, he's largely responsible for my career. He is the individual who advocated the strongest for my first book to be published by Gage House. Now I need his help again . . . my next book I propose to be quite different than what I've done so far, and I need someone with Gage's vision to advocate for me again. Even though he has sold the publishing house, he retains a great influence. What he suggests is typically carried out. I want him on my side when I present my next proposal."

"I see. Well, tomorrow, let me take you to see him. I'll stay out of the way and you can talk to him as you need to."

"That's a kind offer, sir."

"I try to be a kind man."

A visit with Gage may have been the plan for the day, but the first stop would be the library at Repentance Creek. The library operated in a better facility than I had anticipated we would find. This, Clelland explained, was due to the largesse of none other than Walter Gage, who had donated almost all the money used to build the structure, which with its gables and broad front porch looked more like a house than a public building. Gage, a true bibliophile, had upon his move to this area been dismayed at the lack of a public library in the county, and had made it his personal mission to correct that deficiency. A plaque hanging by the door told the story.

I looked forward to talking to Walter Gage and telling him of my hopes for my next novel . . . a novel that would be somewhat daring from the commercial perspective in that it would break the pattern of my earlier books by not relating to the war or to Andersonville nearly so directly. It would instead be the story of the early life of the central character in my second novel, showing his progress toward the events in that book and how the experiences of childhood foreshadowed what would happen to him as an adult. There would be resistance to this change of approach at the publishing house; I would need the influence of Gage to overcome the hesitance to tread on different ground.

The day was growing warm already; I

sweated beneath the fresh bandage Rosalita had provided me that morning. The woman was amazing, able to do anything, it seemed; I felt as secure in her care as I would under the supervision of the finest physician in some huge and progressive city. My wound, beginning to heal already, had also begun to itch. Rosalita had promised to put together a salve she said would end the itching; she would apply it the next time she changed the bandage. I could hardly wait for the relief.

"I never spent much time in libraries, got to admit," Charlie Crowder said as we dismounted in front of a hitchpost near the library. "It's a strain for me to read . . . never had much good schooling."

"I encourage you to read all you can, Charles," said Clelland. "Now that you've met an author, that should give you all the more inspiration to do so. Perhaps you might wish to read one of Jed's novels."

"Maybe, sometime or another." Crowder craned his neck and looked through the library window. "Gentlemen, there is a very lovely woman on the other side of that window."

Clelland took a look. "Yes, indeed . . . that's Mrs. Stover, who operates the library."

"So she's a missus . . . ain't it always the

way? The pretty ones are always married."

"She's widowed," said Clelland. "Her husband was the local schoolmaster for a couple of years. A weak and sickly man. He died almost a year ago, some kind of fever."

"Sad story."

"Yep . . . but one that creates hopeful options for local bachelors."

"Think a schoolmaster's widow would ever have anything to do with a cowboy?" Crowder asked.

"Why, you never know, Charlie," Clelland said.

Like Crowder, I couldn't tear my eyes off the vision on the other side of the rather dark window. This was a woman of beauty worthy of a stage. "Forget cowboys," I said. "I would think a librarian might have more in common with an author."

"Now, that sounds like a likely connection," said Clelland.

Crowder gave me an evil eye. "You and me are thinking about picking apples in the same orchard, I think."

"It's an open orchard as far as I am aware," I said.

"Well, when she chooses me, I hope you'll have the grace to bow out."

"You're a self-confident SOB, Charlie Crowder."

79

"Just irresistably appealing to women, that's all."

We walked to the door; Clelland opened it and led the way in.

"Mrs. Stover!" he said. "How are you faring today?"

Her voice had the clear ring of a crystal bell, perfectly suiting her beauty. "I suppose I'm doing well enough, Mr. Clelland."

"You don't sound very sure of it."

"I'm distressed by some gossip I heard at the cafe this morning, at breakfast. There was a stagecoach robbery, these men were saying, and three people killed, including poor David Flynn . . . they say it will all be in today's paper. I hope it isn't true!"

Clelland leaned against the checkout desk. "Sorry to say it, Mrs. Stover, but it is true. The coach was robbed by Tate Barco and his partner Hiram Canty . . . and three were indeed killed, including David Flynn. And now Canty is dead, too, apparently killed by his own partner."

"Dear God!" She had gone pale.

"Ma'am, are you all right?" Crowder asked.

"Just shocked, that's all. I knew David Flynn quite well . . . he was in here frequently."

Clelland reached over and patted her

80

forearm gently. It was somewhat forward, maybe, given that he'd just met her, but he did it in a natural and inoffensive way.

"I'd like you to meet some friends of mine," Clelland said. "This here is Charlie Crowder, a local man working in the cattle business . . . you may have seen him around town."

"Yes, I've seen him," she said, giving Charlie a smile that could melt butter.

"And this man here is new to our region, but I feel certain you've encountered his name before, given that you are a librarian. This is Mr. Jed Wells, author of two noted novels, and many more to come."

She looked at me differently. "Jed Wells . . . 'The Dark Stockade,' 'The Lost Man?' *That* Jed Wells?"

"Those are my titles," I said.

The smile she gave me was even warmer than what Charlie Crowder had received. She looked prettier by the moment.

Clelland said, "Mrs. Stover, Jed and Charlie are lending a hand to Sheriff Strickland — whose life Jed saved from an assassin, by the way — in investigating the stage robbery and killings. And regarding David Flynn in particular . . . there was a portrait found among his possessions. We wondered if you might know the person portrayed."

We showed her the portrait of the unidentified girl.

"I don't know her."

"You sure about that, ma'am?" Clelland asked. "Because I feel nearly certain that I've seen her in town, and in fact here in this library."

She cocked her head in apparent surprise, and perhaps a touch of offense at this questioning of her truthfulness. "Perhaps she was in here at some time . . . but I don't recall her, and don't know her."

"When I saw her, she was shelving books off that rolling cart. As if working here," Charlie said confidently.

She gave him a cockeyed, forced smile. "I assure you, if she worked here, I would know it."

"I would assume you would."

"We believe she was a friend of David Flynn," I said, "given that he had that picture with him."

Mrs. Stover looked at the portrait again. "She is quite a pretty girl . . . maybe David didn't know her, but admired her beauty and kept the portrait for that reason."

"Why do you say that?"

"Because he never spoke to me about a girl. He would have told me if he had such a relationship."

"You were close friends, then."

"We were close friends."

"Might he have perceived you as more than a friend? If so, that would explain why he never mentioned this girl to you."

"No . . . David is — was — younger than I. He was under no illusions that we were more than two people fond of one another in a friendly way. But David did have some romantic involvements over the years . . . there was a young woman a couple of years ago he held strong interest in, but I'm afraid it was an unrequited love . . . and it was not the young woman in the portrait."

I talked to her awhile longer — no headway made in identifying the girl in the portrait, though. Charlie hung around, looking with admiration at the beautiful librarian, but saying little.

6

Outside the library, though, Charlie grabbed me by the shoulder and turned me around to face him so fast that it caused the heavy bandage on my head to move, bringing pain. He looked into my wincing face, solemnly. Clelland was gone, heading for a clothing store as soon as we left the library. A desperate need for some new pants, he'd told us.

"You know she was lying, don't you?" Charlie said to me.

"About what?"

"About the girl, the portrait. Her eyes showed it — she knows that girl, Jed."

"Why would she lie?"

"Maybe she is trying to protect the girl from something . . . harassment, trouble."

A glint of light from across the street drew my eye to big window of the Repentance Creek General Mercantile Store. The glint was a flash of sunlight from the barrel of a rifle that was part of a display of firearms for sale. A sign hanging inside the window declared that the guns were provided by the Cormondy Gun Shop of Merritt.

Inside the store, Crowder and I studied the assorted rifles.

"You know, Charlie, I can't describe how much I resent the theft of my rifle. Compared to the murders, that is just a small part of Barco's crime . . . but it cuts deep for me. That rifle has been with me through some of the hardest years of my life. And it was a gift from my father, which is what makes it matter most. I want that rifle back, and I want Barco to pay for taking it, and for everything else he did."

"So do I, Jed. The man's a devil in human form."

"A local man, Barco is?"

"No, no, not to start with. Came down here from Indiana or some other such I-starting place. Maybe Illinois. He could have gone anywhere in the country, and here's where he chose to come. Ain't we lucky!"

"What drew him here?"

"Lord, I don't know. Maybe he just felt like law enforcement here wouldn't be as strong as other places. Or maybe he liked the scenery. I have no idea, Jed."

A man in armbands and a clerk's apron walked over. "Can I get some of those rifles out of the rack for you?" he asked.

"Hello, Buster. I'd like to see that Winchester," said Charlie. "Jed, meet one of Repentance Creek's finest merchants, Buster Butler."

"Hello, Buster. Pleased to meet you."

Buster, who seemed a simple fellow, pumped my hand with enthusiasm and grinned broadly at Charlie. "Charlie, I hear there's going to be quite a story in the newspaper today," he said. "As I'm told it, you and some other folk very nearly rid us of Tate Barco once and for all."

"Is that what's being said?"

"That's what I've heard."

"The truth is, Barco got the best of us more than us getting the best of him. He killed poor old David Flynn and the coach driver and guard, and wounded Jed here with a grazing shot."

"I'm not bad hurt," I threw in.

"Good, sir. I'm glad to hear it." He pulled a key from his pocket and unlocked the gun rack. He pulled off a Winchester lever-action and handed it to Charlie. To me he said, "May I get one down for you, sir?"

"I've already got a rifle, though at the moment it is stolen."

86

"Well, should you want to replace it, I hope you'll allow me to help you out."

"I will. But for now, Mr. Clelland has given me use of a borrowed rifle, and I'll be content with that."

"It's my hope that someday Barco will be gunned down, as he deserves . . . and if the gun that did it came from my store, it would be a point of pride for me the rest of my days."

"How much do you know about Barco, Mr. Butler?" I asked.

"Same things as most other folks, I guess. Mostly that he's rubbish with feet."

"Do you know why he chooses to live here in these parts?"

"I've heard it rumored he has relatives here."

"Really?" Charlie said. "I've never heard that."

"I don't recall where I heard it . . . probably just somebody in the store talking out of the top of their head."

Reliable or not, the notion of Barco relatives in the vicinity could make sense of what had drawn him here. And it could provide avenues to find him . . . perhaps he was even hiding out in the home of a relation. I'd talk about it to the sheriff when I got a chance.

We looked at the rifle awhile longer, then went out back and took a few shots with it on a target range out back. Charlie had me test it for accuracy, and I gave it high marks. Charlie bought the rifle, putting half of it onto a credit account already established at the store. We left with me wishing all the more that I had my lost rifle back again.

In midafternoon, I saw a boy of about 12 come around a corner with a stack of newspapers in a wagon he pulled behind him. A crowd gathered quickly; newspaper sales were brisk today, and I could easily guess why.

Charlie got to the boy first and bought a copy for himself and one for me. The story led the front page, just like I'd expected. What I hadn't expected was an accompanying set of illustrations. Pembrook Jones was an artist as well as a writer.

One of the illustrations, quite fanciful but relatively accurate at the same time, showed a man who looked something like me taking a shot to the side of the head inside a stagecoach. It was Jones's creative vision of the moment I was wounded. His sketches were sufficiently good for me to identify each of my fellow passengers. The rendering of Charlie Crowder was particularly accurate, but Charlie didn't think so.

"I'm not such a scrawny runt as that!" he bellowed, slapping at the paper with the back of a hand. "He drew me as no thicker around than that porch post there!"

"You're a slender fellow, Charlie," I said. "And he's not distorted you as much as you're acting like he did. Look at the picture again — not bad for someone who wasn't there. Let's just hope he is as accurate in his writing as in his drawing."

We headed into the shade behind a livery stable and sat down on an old bench there, leaning back against an oak. Unfolding the newspapers, we began to read, one or the other of us occasionally throwing in a comment as we went.

I was not surprised by what I found, because I'd expected Jones to do a good job, but I was gratified to have that expectation fulfilled. Jones had done a fine piece of journalism, accurately conveying the sequence of events and a surprising number of the fine details.

Then I reached the portion that recounted my shooting of the man who had tried to assassinate the sheriff. Again the journalism was accurate in detail — even more so than the discussion of the stagecoach robbery because Jones had had the advantage of being an eyewitness to this part — but I was embarrassed by the veneer of heroism in which he enwrapped me through his story. I was presented as the "valiant rescuer of Rabun County's greatest knight of law, Sheriff Guy Strickland, he of Ranger fame." And in killing Bailey Freeman, I had "dealt a blow against the suffering of innocent women who are tormented under the assaults of heartless men who dare to raise a fist against that which God gave Adam as helpmeet and companion." Bailey, in Jones's estimation, was hardly human, simply a beast, worth shooting simply because of the way he treated his wife and children.

In this presentation, Jones showed himself to be quite a progressive thinker. The attitude of many men, perhaps most, was that wives were possessions, property of a man in much the same way as a dog or a calf . . . and too many believed that on occasion, any wife deserved a beating. Even the law generally failed to defend the right of women not to be abused by their own husbands. In even answering the call to the Freeman home, the sheriff had done more than most in his place would have done, and more than many officers would have done in that situation.

When Charlie reached the portion of the story describing Bailey Freeman's death, he read with a frown on his face, then looked at me with head shaking from side to side. "This isn't a good thing for you, my friend," he said. "You may live to regret having shot Bailey in the presence of a man who buys ink in barrels."

"What's so bad in what he's written?"

"What's bad is something *not* written in that story, but it will be in Bailey's obituary, I can tell you. He's got family. Brothers, a father who is meaner than Satan's schoolmaster, and cousins all as foul and mean as he is."

"You believe they'll come after me?"

"I'd bet everything I have on it . . . though in respect for you, I won't actually start betting on your death."

"You honestly believe I should be worried?"

"Yes. That's a rough family, Jed. And now they'll know who you are . . . and it won't help that they were all Rebs during the war."

This I fully understood. Jones had given a fairly complete biography of me in his story, much of which I recognized as coming from the biography page published with my novels. So now the Freemans and everyone else who read this paper knew exactly who had fired the bullet that killed Bailey Freeman. And that I was described in such heroic terms for having fired it could only fuel their inevitable bitterness and resentment, as would the fact I now made my living writing books that did not present the late Confederacy in flattering terms.

If the other Freemans approached retribution in the backshooting manner Bailey had, then I might face a sharpshooter's ultimate irony: death by a shot fired from hiding.

It came to mind right then that perhaps my best decision would be to find Walter Gage as quickly as I could, complete my business with him, and leave Texas right away. Let Strickland and the locals deal with bringing Barco to justice. This was not my place in the world, nor my role in life.

But I couldn't forget that David Flynn had died because Tate Barco had missed the shot he fired at me. This was my fight whether I liked it or not. If the wrath of the Freeman family created an additional hazard for me, I would simply have to endure it.

Neither Charlie nor I had eaten since we left Clelland's house that morning, and Charlie suggested we have a meal at a particular cafe of which he was fond. At that point I'd have gladly eaten out of one of the stable feed troughs, so I agreed at once to Charlie's idea.

We found a table beside the front window, which was made in one of those common checkerboard red-and-white patterns. The tablecloth matched the window.

A waiter in a faded, food-stained suit came our way, looking quite bored. But when he spotted my bandage, then apparently recognized Charlie Crowder, a light of interest came into his eyes and lit his entire face. Another reader of the RABUN COUNTY ADVOCATE, obviously. He came to the table and spoke hesitantly.

"Hello, sirs . . . howdy, Charlie."

"Howdy, Joe."

The waiter had turned his head toward Charlie, but his eyes were turned toward me. "I read about you in the newspaper," he said.

"I didn't even know you could read, Joe."

"I learnt last year. Janie Flatt taught me."

"Janie? She's a mighty pretty girl, Joe! How'd you persuade such a pretty thing to stick her head into a book with a homely old hoss like you long enough to teach you to read?"

"Told her I wanted to learn to read so I could read the Bible. She's religious, you know, and wants to make other folks religious, too."

"So she decided to spend time with a bug

93

like you for the sake of saving your soul."

"I guess that's it." He grinned, and for the first time since he'd come up looked squarely at me. "Hello, sir. I reckon you must be the Mister Jed Wells who saved the life of our sheriff and also made a valiant shot intended to kill Tate Barco."

"I'm Jed Wells . . . pleased to meet you."

"Me, too . . . you're a true hero, sir, and I'm honored to get to speak to you."

"I don't merit such flattering words," I said. "I certainly don't see myself as a hero. All I did was wait too long to fire a shot that missed its mark, anyway. Here's your hero, right across the table! This is the man who climbed out of a moving coach with outlaws in pursuit, and climbed up to the driver's seat."

"Yeah . . . I read that in the paper. Good job, Charlie."

"Why, thank you, Joe. Now, how about you bring us two heroes a couple of steaks. Potatoes and beans, too. And coffee. Have your mother make the coffee, because ain't nobody makes it like her. When you make coffee, Joe, it tastes like you peed in the pot."

"All right, Charlie. I'll have Mama make it. And by the way, because of what you done, both of you, there's no cost to you for this meal."

"You needn't do that," I protested.

"No, no . . . it's something we like to do here, in such special situations."

"It would be rude of us to refuse it," Charlie said.

"We are honored, then," I said. "Thank you, Joe."

7

By the time the steaks arrived and we began eating, others in the cafe had made the same identification as Joe had, and approached our table. To our good fortune, all had a positive view of what Charlie and I had done to gain local fame, and I actually grew tired of thanking people for their kind comments and congratulations. I asked those who came to us a few questions about Barco, where he'd come from, where he lived, and whether he had any known local relatives, but answers were uninformative.

Charlie had become the unofficial guardian of the portrait from the blue carpetbag, and after the third admiring visitor came to our table, he brought it out and asked that visitor if he had seen this girl before. The fellow looked at the picture blankly, but Joe the cafe waiter happened to come up behind him at that moment, coffee pot in hand for the refreshment of our cups, and saw the picture. In Joe's eyes I saw the light of recognition.

"I don't know her, sir," the visitor to our table said.

Joe stepped around and nearly in front of him. "Why are you carrying around Merry's picture?" he asked Charlie.

"Mary?" Charlie asked. "Is that her name?"

"Yes. She spells it M-E-R-R-Y, as in 'happy,' rather than the usual way. Don't ask me why."

"Who is she?"

"Merry Gavin. She lives in a little house about half a mile south of town . . . if you headed out that road there and just kept going, you'd go right past it."

"Is she married, live with her parents, or what?" I asked.

"She lives alone — her parents are dead, but some relative lives right next door to her and keeps an eye on her."

"Does Merry Gavin work at the local library?" I asked Joe.

"Yes, sir, she does. I've seen her going in and out of there many a time."

So Mrs. Stover had indeed lied to us. But why?

"Thank you for the information, Joe," I said.

"You're welcome, sir." With that, he wandered off.

"She did lie to us, Charlie."

"Yeah, she surely did."

"Why would she do that?"

"Well, Jed, let's think about this a little," he said. "How much do we really know? Not a lot. We now know with a good deal of certainty that this pretty Gavin gal works at the library, and that Mrs. Stover, for whatever reason, didn't want us to know that. But we don't know that there is a connection between the girl and the things that happened to David Flynn."

"You're right."

"But there's something about that picture of her that nags at me. I want to ask you about it, but let me see that picture again before I shoot my mouth off like a fool."

I handed him the Merry Gavin portrait and he moved around a little to get it in the best light. Then he leaned over and squinted at it.

"Yeah, I still see it."

"What?"

"The resemblance. This gal looks like somebody else I'm thinking of . . . like they could be family with one another." He held the portrait out for me to look at.

"Who are you thinking she looks like?

Mrs. Stover? Because they are both mighty pretty women, but not kin that we are aware of."

"It ain't Mrs. Stover she resembles. Somebody different than that . . . somebody you wouldn't expect. I may be letting my imagination run off on me, Jed, or maybe I'm going loco . . . I don't know. But look at her eyes, and think where you've seen eyes like that before."

I pulled back a little to allow my increasingly far-sighted eyes a better look at the pretty image . . . and all at once I saw what Charlie meant. She reminded me of someone, too, but for the life of me I couldn't remember who. If it was the same person Charlie was thinking of, though, it had be someone in this region, someone Charlie and I had both seen — but that narrowed the field of possibilities radically. How many people here had both I and Charlie crossed paths with? I began a mental run-down of faces, starting with those at the stage depot and then on the stage itself.

To my surprise, I found the face I was looking for quickly, and it was like a kick in the stomach.

"Charlie," I said, "I know who she looks like."

He squinted at me, a wry expression. "Are

we thinking of the same person?" I asked.

"A man . . . not a woman?"

"Right."

"A man we both saw yesterday morning . . . one who left you with a furrow plowed down the side of your head?"

"That's the very man I'm thinking of, Charlie. Those eyes of hers . . . those are the eyes of Tate Barco himself!"

It sounded awfully farfetched as I said it, but a mere glance back down at the portrait reconfirmed what my own eyes had told me. The resemblance between Merry Gavin and Tate Barco was so striking that I could not believe it was merely coincidental.

Charlie's mind was running on similar lines, obviously, as his words revealed. "Let's let ourselves think some loco thoughts here, Jed. Just to see where they lead us. Let's imagine for a minute that this Gavin gal is Barco's daughter, hiding under a different name out of shame over her father's wickedness. Now let's also suppose that David Flynn was in love with her, and knew who she really was . . . and that his daddy knew as well. Wouldn't that do a lot to drive a father and son apart? Especially with the father being a banker. That would mean that David Flynn was courting the very daughter of the outlaw who robbed the father's banks?"

It did sound plausible, and I said as much. But there were some big leaps being made. Especially in labeling Merry Gavin as Barco's daughter based on a perceived resemblance between her and the outlaw.

"One question, Charlie: why would Mrs. Stover lie to us about Merry working at the library?"

Charlie nodded and went on. "Now, bear with me here. Imagine that you're a widow woman in a small town like Repentance Creek, and you've got a pretty young gal, all alone, working for you. You'd naturally want to protect this gal. Now, imagine that a terrible thing happens, people getting robbed and killed, and all at once folks are coming around looking for the young gal, and you don't know exactly what they are thinking or what might come of it for her. What might you do? You might lie to protect her, that's what. Mrs. Stover probably didn't know what kind of trouble we might bring to Merry. So she just decided to keep us apart, if she could. Let the whole thing blow over and die down, and keep the gal out of it as much as possible. That's why she lied to us, I'll betcha!"

"But it's not a lie that can be carried on for long. Too many people know Merry works there and can refute what Mrs. Stover said."

"Well, maybe she didn't figure we'd push the matter long enough for that to happen. I mean, we ain't law officers, not really, anyway. Just a couple of fill-in temporary deputies, that's all."

"You're probably right. Hey, though, tell me something: what is Mrs. Stover's first name?"

"Anne."

"Anne Stover. Pretty name. I wonder what her name was before she married that schoolmaster?"

"I don't know."

"Speaking of marriage, if Merry Gavin really is daughter to Tate Barco, then there must be a Mrs. Barco somewhere."

"You ain't suggesting that would be Anne Stover, are you?"

"Lord, no! But there's a mother somewhere. Got to be."

"Yes . . . but not necessarily a Mrs. Barco as such. Tate Barco wouldn't think twice about consorting outside the bonds of matrimony. He's not a high and moral type of man."

"You're right about that, no question. But she must not be around now, or else Merry Gavin wouldn't live alone."

"Maybe her mother is dead. Maybe Barco is a widower," Charlie conjectured. "I've never heard a wife mentioned in connection with him."

"What if it really is only coincidence that Merry and Barco bear a resemblance?"

"Then you and me have been mightily fooled. But it strains the mind to believe such similarity is just chance."

I studied the picture some more and saw Charlie was right. "I'll say this: those eyes look a lot prettier peeping out of her head than Tate Barco's."

"Ain't *that* the truth!" Charlie pulled out a cigar and lighted it. "How you reckon that wickedness and beauty can run in the same family that way?"

"I guess one has nothing to do with the other," I said.

"That's a good point, Jed. The wickedest human being I ever knowed was also one of the finest to look at. I'm speaking of the late Carmen Potts, of the town of Merritt."

"Your woman?" I asked, wishing Charlie would offer me a cigar, too. I stared at his in a way I hoped he'd notice.

"She was . . . I was going to marry her. But she was unfaithful to me. That's the wickedness I'm talking about. Us not even married, me still believing her pure and

103

unsullied, and trying to respect that no matter how tempted I was to move in on her . . . and then she goes and climbs in the barn loft with a dang Mexican trail cook. Good Lord, I nearly died when I learned of it. She even bore his baby, that woman did! Named it some Mexican name or another and sent it off with its daddy to go back to Mexico so they could raise it Catholic, because the father insisted on it. I don't take to that Catholic business, myself — all those statues and ceremonies and tall hats and funny-sounding words. I'm a Baptist . . . except for Baptists not drinking. To that degree I ain't much Baptist."

"I'm sorry to hear about what happened with your bride-to-be. Unfaithfulness brings a lot of pain."

"Better it happened before the wedding than after, huh? That's how I try to look at it."

"You're a philosophical man, Charlie."

"Just stupid and unlucky, that's all. One who picked a woman who was even more stupid, and more unlucky."

"You'll do better next time. Any woman would be lucky to hook you on her line, Charlie Crowder."

"We'll see. You know, Jed, I'm surprised you ain't settled down and married by now."

"Got to meet the right woman to do that. I ain't met her yet."

"Maybe you have, and just don't realize who she is yet."

"You wouldn't be talking about a certain librarian, would you?"

"Lord, no! I'm talking about *your* woman, not mine!"

"So Anne Stover is your woman now?"

"She might be!"

Outside a big, dark, horse-drawn conveyance, covered with flowers and crepe, rolled past on the street, drawn by four horses and driven by a man in a black suit and matching top hat.

"What the devil is that?" I exclaimed.

"It's the undertaker's hearse, the bigger of the two that he has, in fact. The one he saves for special occasions, like double funerals."

"Double?"

"Our driver and our guard . . . cousins, they were. The relatives decided to say words over both of them together and drop them in their holes at the same time."

"Why not just throw in David Flynn and get them all taken care of at once?"

Charlie laughed. "That would never happen, Jed. Not with Albert Flynn still lording around. If you know him, you'd know his boy would never be funeralized with a couple of common stagecoach crewmen. The common rabble are just that to Albert Flynn . . . though I don't think David himself was prone to such uppity thinking."

"I despise a man with his nose in the air," I said.

"Good for you, Jed. For you could easily be that way yourself, if you let yourself think about all you've done. Books that everybody wants to read . . . success at war and at peace both — you've got more to stick up your nose about than any Flynn ever will."

"Thank you, Charlie. But I don't see my life in the same way you do."

"That's because you're humble, and that's a good thing, too."

"Well, say whatever good you want about me, there's one thing you *can't* say: it wasn't me who had the courage to climb out on the side of a moving coach, with outlaws closing in."

"Why, that wasn't no stunt a monkey couldn't have done."

"I don't recall any monkeys being on that stagecoach to do it."

"I don't know . . . Estella Dupont kind of looks like one."

"Charlie, shame on you! She seems a kind, sweet woman, and reminds me of my

106

own mother. Don't talk about her that way!"

"Beg pardon, Mr. Politeness."

I grinned and glanced out the window. The hearse was rolling to a stop in front of a big church with a tall steeple. A crowd was already gathering there, women in black dresses, men in black or deep gray suits, and quite a few in lesser attire, the garb of common working folks. I thought something that only later, in retrospect, would seem an odd and somewhat grim thought: these were the kind of people I would want to come to my own funeral, many years from now, I hoped. These were the people whose appreciation mattered to me. Not the Albert Flynns of the world, with their arrogance and pomposity.

"Maybe we should go over there for the services," I said. "We were with them when they died, after all."

"I had a similar thought," Charlie said. "We ain't in chuchhouse clothes, but a lot of folks going in ain't dressed up, either."

"Let's go pay respects, then."

8

We walked to the church, drawing attention as we proceeded. After the publication of Pembrook Jones' story, the bandage poking out from under my hat was like a badge of identification.

"Wells!" a stranger yelled. "It's the man who nearly killed Tate Barco!"

Men and boys crowded around me and Charlie, pumping our hands, slapping our shoulders . . . strange, really. Some of the men had tear-streaked faces, being friends or relations of the two dead men waiting in the church, but beamed bright smiles at Charlie and me.

Over beside the church well, though, stood a group of heavy-set men, all smoking, glaring at me through piggish eyes. Several had red hair, and I realized that I was looking at kin of the late Bailey Freeman, a group that surely held a less flattering view of my recent exploits than did most hereabouts. I stood in a way to keep that group in the corner of my eye at all times. It came to mind that this group probably had already been to one funeral today, or would attend another later, laying away one of their own, the man I had killed.

"I regret that we were unable to save the lives of your friends," I said to the admirers around me. "They were good men who tried hard to keep their passengers safe. Tate Barco should hang for what he did."

"String him up and I'll swing from his ankles while he's hanging there!" a tow-headed little boy said, his high voice rising up below. "I'll stretch his neck for him good!"

"That's the spirit, Billy boy!" a man beside the boy said, rubbing the lad's hair. I pictured the boy doing what he'd said, and felt sickened. I despised Tate Barco and believed he'd earned himself a death sentence, but seeing grown men praising little boys for murderous fantasies was distressing.

Charlie seemed much more comfortable with all this than I was. He knew several of the men around and talked friendly banter with them, moving on quickly to a very dramatic recounting of the adventure on the stagecoach. It wasn't self-serving though; in Charlie's telling, I was the hero of the day, himself no more than a clumsy assistant at best. I tried to clarify the facts and expand upon Charlie's role, but this was Charlie's audience, and they clearly took his self-efacing version of the facts over mine.

The group drifted toward the church-house door, but I let myself fall back to the rear. My head hurt and itched under the bandage, and I wished I had Rosalita handy to change the dressing and anoint me with some of her magical salve.

Typically, the rear portion of the sanctuary filled more quickly than the front. I found the last space on the last pew in the central block of pews and parked myself there. Seated behind a tall, Lincolnesque fellow with curly hair, I had only a limited view of the front of the church and the two closed coffins placed there on tables. The church was packed with mourners; the widows and children of the deceased were in a special area at the front, and made for a piteous sight. Just good, common folk, left bereaved because of the wickedness of two highwaymen. It made me want Barco's hide all the more.

The service began with hymns — slow, mournful numbers about death and parting. A mood of even deeper depression settled over the assembly. Charlie Crowder, seated three pews up from me, writhed like a schoolboy in a boring class and looked like a man wishing he'd not come in. When a new hymn of misery and suffering began, I turned my eye toward the back door, which stood wide open to allow at least some circulation of air in this crowded sanctuary. Seated where I was, I could be out that door in only a moment. All that restrained me was a sense that it would be improper to leave just yet.

I forced my attention back to the front of the church and the songleader, who stood in his black suit, waving his hand in time to the music and sweating profusely all along his broad forehead. He blinked as the stinging sweatdrops trickled through his thick brows down into his eyes, and he had his eye on the back door, too, though it was far out of his reach.

I glanced out the door again to welcome a cool breeze that found its way in, and saw, on down the street, another hearse slowly rolling along, pulled by a smaller team. It was headed into the yard of another church, one that was very classically styled and had a huge sign declaring it the meeting place of the local Episcopalian congregation. A

111

man was walking slowly along beside the hearse, a handkerchief in hand. As I watched, he dabbed his eyes with the handkerchief.

He was a goodly distance away, but even from here I found he reminded me a lot of David Flynn. Surely I was looking at Albert Flynn, father of David. David's funeral surely would also be held today, apparently over at that Episcopal church.

The hymn ended and a prayer commenced, just as mournful as the music. That was it — my decision was made.

Moving quietly and quickly, I slipped into the aisle, angled off to the right, and was out the door in less than four seconds. The cool air outside the church was invigorating.

Flynn saw me coming when I was halfway to him. He wiped that handkerchief across his brow and cocked his head a little, as if maybe one of his eyes was stronger than the other and he wanted to study me with that one. I'd taken off my hat when I entered the church a few minutes earlier, but had put it back on after my escape. Approaching the hearse and coffin, I took it off again. I saw Flynn looking closely at my bandage. He thrust out his hand as I reached him. "Mr. Jed Wells, I presume?" he said.

"Yes, sir. And you are Mr. Albert Flynn, father of David?"

"I am," he said, pumping my hand. "And I am a man in sorrow right now, but also in gratitude for those who sought to avert the tragedy that has struck me and mine. I read of your courageous acts in the newspaper."

"I don't know that my acts were extraordinarily courageous, and the fact is, they didn't work to save your son. Sir, I'm obliged to tell you that I believe the bullet that ended David's life was intended for me, and that had I been a more effective sharpshooter, I might have staved off this loss to your family."

"You did what you could, sir, and that is what rouses my gratitude. It is not because of you that David died. It is because of Tate Barco, and because of David's own poor judgment long before his path and yours crossed."

I had no inkling what he meant; surely he was touching the edges of whatever matter had estranged him from David.

"Mr. Flynn, though I didn't know David, having only met him at the time we caught the same stagecoach, I have heard good things about him from some who knew him. Mrs. Estella Dupont in particular held him in high regard."

"Ah, yes, Estella . . . a fine woman, married to a fine man now lost to us. She loved David . . . I think for her he was a sort of replacement for the son she lost during the hostilities of the '60s."

"She told me about her son while we rode together. I also heard good things regarding your own son from another woman who considered him a friend — Mrs. Anne Stover, the librarian."

His look changed as I called that name. His eyes narrowed and his mouth clamped closed into a tight, tense line. "Ah, yes . . . the lovely Mrs. Stover. How kind of her to speak well of my boy, given the associations of her own family."

"I've lost your meaning, sir," I said.

"Please pardon me if it all sounds cryptic . . . it is difficult for you, a stranger to this town, to be thrust into circumstances with a history long preceding your arrival. Because of my gratitude to and admiration for you, Mr. Wells, I'll be forthright and tell you that my loss of David came at a time when he and I were of very different minds . . . estranged from one another, in fact. And the cause of it all had to do with David's poor choice of those with whom he chose to entangle himself."

"Mr. Flynn, none of this is my affair

except to the extent that witnessing David's tragic death, and knowing that I had at least a peripheral and indirect involvement in it, has roused a deep personal interest on my part in seeing justice done to those guilty. Even so, I hope you will allow me to inquire with you about something, and know that my intrusions into your family's affairs come from nothing but the best motivations."

"I can easily believe that, Mr. Wells. Ask me what you will."

I had retained the portrait of Merry Gavin at the cafe, and with some sense of trepidation took it from my pocket. "This was found among David's possessions after the robbery," I said, opening it and showing it to Flynn. "Also found were several bank note wrappers from the Repentance Creek Bank . . . and some strange things were said." I recounted for him the bandits' words about "getting back" the contents of the blue carpetbag, which we now knew was money. The implication of "getting back" that money was obvious: it was money the thieves had at one point had, then lost — then regained. Which further implied that David Flynn, somehow, had on his person during that last stagecoach ride money that had come from Barco and Canty. Could it have been some of the money they had taken in the robbery of the bank? Whatever its origin, how had David Flynn gotten his hands on it, and where was he taking it at the time he was killed?

Albert Flynn looked at the portrait of Merry Gavin, then fired a harsh glare up at me. "This is not a face I wish to see on the day I'm laying my son to his final rest," he said, his voice a kind of growl.

"Who is she?" I asked, playing slightly more ignorant than I was.

"The offspring of filth and vermin, that's who she is!"

"That's a strong statement, sir. What is her name?"

"Merry Gavin, though by all rights she should use a different last name. This, sir, is the daughter of none other than Tate Barco."

"I do see a facial resemblance."

"This young woman, sir, is the reason my son is dead today. Had he never met her, had he never allowed her to influence him to the most unwise, and I have to say, most illegal and immoral activities in connection with her father's criminal activities, the circumstances that set the stage for his murder would not have happened."

"I was told by Mrs. Stover at the library

that David was in love with that young woman."

"Yes, it's true . . . even if said by such as her."

"Why do you hold Mrs. Stover in such low regard?"

"Why should I not despise the woman who encouraged my son's relationship with the daughter of Tate Barco?"

"She encouraged that?"

"Very strongly. The girl is her niece, you know."

That was another jolt. "I *didn't* know. Does that mean that Mrs. Stover also is related to Tate Barco?"

"Not by blood. Her husband's sister, now deceased, was Tate Barco's wife. Not legally his wife, by the way, but simply joined to him through the common law. She was the widow of a man named Gavin when she associated herself with Barco. That illegitimate union gave rise to Merry Gavin, who was raised for the most part by her aunt, Anne Stover, rather than by her true mother. No doubt Anne Stover, despite my lack of regard for her, was at least a better guardian than her true mother would have been."

"Sir, when we inquired of Mrs. Stover regarding the girl, she denied that the girl worked with her in the library, even though

I learned since that she does work there. I can guess only that she was in some way trying to protect Merry . . . do you know any other reason she would deny such a fact?"

"I neither know nor care."

He looked at the shining hearse, reached over, and rubbed his hand along the paneled side. The handkerchief went up to his eyes again. However unlikable he was, this was a man to be pitied, a man truly suffering in his bereavement.

"Mr. Flynn, let me present to you something that occurred in the course of the robbery that left me puzzled."

"Go ahead."

I told him then about the intensity with which his son had guarded the carpetbag, and about how Barco and Canty had reacted when they realized David Flynn was dead. Without belaboring details, I told him even of their contemptuous actions toward David's corpse.

"As best I can put it together, your son must have managed to get back some of the money stolen by Barco and Canty when they robbed your bank. He must have been bringing it back at the time they struck the stagecoach. Maybe they even knew that he was doing that . . . maybe that's what led

118

them to rob that particular coach," I told Flynn.

Flynn took on a deeply pained expression. "Dear God . . . how is a man supposed to understand a life that hands him so many sorrows and mysteries?"

"I don't know what to say to that, Mr. Flynn."

He paused, staring at me in silence, then said, "I'm going to tell you something, sir, that is not easy for me to share. I have alluded to it only indirectly up until now. It is painful and personal, and involves the most hurtful betrayal I have ever suffered."

"Sir, you need not tell me anything that would cause you more grief."

"I want to do so . . . I want you to understand the context of the situation between myself and my late son. We did not get on well in recent times, he and I. Much of it had to do with his choice of a lady friend . . . this worthless girl here." He waved the portrait. "Much of it had to do with a basic difference in attitude and personality between the two of us. I sought to make David take more seriously the need for a man to attain material security in his life. I have been able to do that through my own hard work and wise choices, as my father was able to do the same before me.

David, though, took it all too much for granted. He seemed to resent my success . . . to resent the very source of his own comfortable, secure life. Can you make sense of something like that, Mr. Wells?"

"No, sir . . . but I've heard of such things happening in many fine families."

"I loved my son, Mr. Wells. I don't know whether he himself always was persuaded of it, or whether I showed it enough, but I did love him. He grew to so resent me, though, that he let himself fall under the spell of this little witch . . . . here, take back this picture . . . and she was able to persuade him even further against me. She presented to him a most loathsome scheme, a way he could 'avenge' himself against me for all perceived wrongs or shortcomings. The idea ultimately came, I feel sure, from her father, because it benefited him above all others. And David, foolish as he was, and blinded by his ridiculous love for that hussy, agreed to the idea. It hurts like a fire in my heart that he did so, and I think always will."

"What was the scheme, Mr. Flynn?"

He paused a long time, and I thought he'd decided that maybe he was saying too much to me. Then he drew in a deep sigh and continued. "David agreed to help Tate Barco plan a robbery of my bank here in

Repentance Creek . . . that bank over there." He pointed west. "David helped me manage the place, just the day-to-day kinds of operations . . . so it was easy for him to do this. He didn't actually take part in the robbery . . . he simply made sure the situation was right so that Barco and his partner could easily manage the crime. But it took a turn David hadn't anticipated . . . Barco killed a guard, a fine, innocent old fellow who had watched the bank for me for years."

"Mr. Jericho," I said, recalling the name from Estella Dupont's conversation on the stagecoach.

"That's right. Barco shot him down like a dog. It shook David up . . . enough that he confessed to me his part in what had happened. I can tell you, sir, what it feels like to have a hand reach inside you and rip the heart from your chest. I'm sorry to be so dramatic . . . this really is not your affair."

"Sir, it became my concern when I saw your son die. I can't let it go."

Tears streamed down his face and he turned and buried his face in his arms, leaning against the side of the hearse. His shoulders heaved, and he was such a sad character just now that it was easy to forgive him for some of his harsher ways. What did I know of what this man had experienced?

How could I rightly judge him?

I looked down the street and felt my heart do a fast dance inside my ribs. Walking slowly toward Flynn and me was a person I'd never seen before, but knew at once, for her image was burned into my mind.

Even from a distance, Merry Gavin was a striking vision. She wore a long, dark gray dress, a black hat, and carried a ragged parasol, closed and held in her right hand. It was easy to see how David Flynn had been enamored of this young woman. She was breathtaking.

But just now I was not glad to see her. How would Albert Flynn react when he saw her? I dreaded it.

She stopped, having spotted us. She'd recognized Flynn, leaning against the hearse.

She hesitated, then veered leftward, advancing slowly and taking light steps to minimize noise. Her eye caught mine and held for a moment; I could see her trying to decide if she knew me. If she'd read the newspaper, which undoubtedly she had, she'd soon tentatively identify me because of my wounded head.

9

Flynn gained some control of his emotions and straightened, wiping his face with the handkerchief. He wheeled slowly . . . and saw her.

"Dear God!" he exclaimed. *"You* have the gall to come *here?"*

She turned a sad, beautiful face to him. "How could I not come to the funeral of the man I loved?"

He turned to me. "She loved him, she says. Loved him right into his grave!"

"How can you say that?" I asked, honestly appalled. "She had nothing to do with it! She was not even there!"

"Oh, but she caused it, all right! She caused it all, her and her evil father!"

She had heard all of this, and suddenly lunged in our direction, her face now filling with anger. She ignored me and came within ten feet of Flynn before she made herself stop. At first I'd thought she was going to gouge Flynn with that parasol.

"Blame my father, if you want, but don't blame me! I didn't want any of it to happen! I tried to stop them both! It was my father's idea and influence that led David into the scheme . . . not mine! I tried my best to stop it!"

"Not very successful, were you, girl? The bank still got robbed, Mr. Jericho still got killed, and my own son still turned against his own father and helped a thief steal from hundreds of innocent depositors. If you'd wanted to stop it you had only to tell me about it in advance, but you said nothing."

"I didn't want it to happen, Mr. Flynn. I vow it before God! The only reason I said nothing to you was that I wasn't sure David would really go through with such a thing. If I had told you he was considering it, you either would have disbelieved me and dismissed me as a liar, or believed me and despised your son all the more. God knows there was little I could do!"

"How can you even speak the name of God, you foul trollop! You who ruined the life of a young man and his family, and put him in a situation that ended his very life? You even have the blood of old Mr. Jericho on your hands, for you held the power to stop that robbery before it started, yet you held silent! How can you even call God's holy name with such guilt on your dark soul? May he smite you down!"

"How dare you *speak* to me so?" Her eyes welled.

"Would that I never had seen your face, girl! If only David had never known you!" he bellowed at her. "I wish you had never set foot in Texas! I wish your whore of a mother and demon of a father had never given birth to you! Damn your soul, you foul creature! Damn your soul!"

Her face grew very white and full of fear, and her eyes blinked hard as each new burst of abuse hit her. I was as stunned as she. I couldn't keep quiet.

"Mr. Flynn, that's enough of that sort of talk . . . most improper addressed to any woman, no matter how fierce your feelings and emotions," I said. "I insist, in the name of all courtesy and decency, that you speak no more to her in such a harsh manner."

"Don't speak to me so!" he said in a grating voice.

"Then don't speak that way to *her,*" I said.

"I believe you are a good and worthy man, Jed Wells," he said. "This hussy is not worthy of your defense."

"I *will* defend her, sir, as I would defend any woman spoken to so rudely."

125

She asked me, "Sir, are you Mr. Jed Wells, the man I read about in the newspaper?"

"I am," I said. "But let's talk of it another time."

"I do not want you at this funeral service, girl!" Flynn said to her.

"But I must!" she answered. "I loved him in life and I must say my goodbye to him in death."

"You took him from me, hussy! If not for you none of this would have happened! My son would still be alive, and still with me."

"He could never really be with you, Mr. Flynn," she said. "He was too different from you . . . he did not worship money and power as you do! He never would have done so!"

"Money and power, girl, are what drive the world!"

That might have been true, but what drove the hearse bearing the body of David Flynn was a man — someone we all had forgotten about in all this intense conversation. The driver had been slumped in the driver's seat all this time, unmoving and easy to overlook, and when he suddenly rose and climbed down from his perch, he startled us all. Merry actually staggered to the side and looked like she could faint.

He'd heard it all, without question, but

seemed unmoved and indifferent. Not his concern, I guess. "I must move the deceased inside and prepare the church for the service," he said to Flynn.

"Must you be so fast about it?" Flynn asked.

"There is little time left . . . the priest will be here soon, and then the other mourners."

Flynn hung his head. "Go on then, if you must."

The driver scrambled back up to his seat, threw off the brake, and moved the team forward into the alley that ran along the side of the church. The coffin, apparently, would be taken in through the rear, not the front. I wondered how the driver intended to accomplish this alone, then noticed a folded rolling cart of some sort attached to the back of the hearse. Ah, the wonders of human innovation.

Flynn was pathetic again, tears coming as the hearse rolled around the corner. He gave a final glare at Merry Gavin, and walked away, following the hearse. It appeared the driver would have help with the coffin after all.

I was left alone with Merry Gavin. "I'm very sorry about the things he said to you," I told her. "Quite rude . . . unforgivable."

"He is wrong to blame me . . . I did *not* turn the son against his father, despite what he believes. Albert Flynn caused that on his own. David was never like him, and the two of them fought over so many things, trivial and otherwise."

"I'd like to ask you to tell me exactly what happened regarding the robbery of the Repentance Creek Bank," I told her. "David's part, Tate Barco's part, and how David happened to have money from that robbery with him on the stagecoach when we were robbed. Will you tell me that?"

"Yes . . . because you seem a fair man, and because the newspaper says you tried to stop the stagecoach robbery, I'll tell you."

Tried to stop it indeed, by taking a shot at her own father. I marveled at just how divided and hateful families could become within themselves.

"Let's go sit down over here, on the steps," I suggested.

Seated beside her, I had to remind myself of her youth and my lack of it. She was an astonishingly appealing young woman . . . David Flynn, unfortunate in so many ways, had at least been fortunate to be loved by one so lovely.

"So I truly am speaking now to the daughter of Tate Barco?" I asked, wanting a direct and blatant verification of this crucial fact.

She nodded and whispered a sad-sounding "Yes."

"I find myself in an uncomfortable position, for I shot at your father . . . would have killed him if I could."

"My father deserves whatever bad things come to him," she said. "He has earned what he receives."

"Truthfully, what he seems to have received is relatively good fortune," I said. "He has been quite a success at his career of crime, from what I am told. And the law seems unable to bring him in."

"How can there be any success in bringing harm and death to others? He is the greatest failure I know . . . and I would do anything if I could only be the child of another . . . not him."

"I'm very sorry for your unhappiness," I told her. "But we are much more than our parentage, and you must not worry over that which cannot be changed. Now, tell me about David and his father."

"David and his father . . . oh, yes. David came to despise Albert Flynn over the past year or so," she said. "You've seen today what a harsh and unpleasant man he can be. He was worse with David, who in his eyes could do no right, make no decision correctly. The longer they were together, the more they grew to despise one another. But I will be fair: I do believe Mr. Flynn loved his son, in a way, but he had no ability to show it. Ironic that today he can weep over his son's loss, but could find no emotion but bitter anger toward him while he was still alive."

"Yes." I thought back on a score of divided families of whom I'd learned through the private messages given to me by the dying victims of Andersonville . . . I remembered how intense was the desire on the part of so many of them to convey healing words to their kin, so that final memories would not be so bitter.

"It was my father, sorry to say, who put forward the idea of David 'avenging' himself against his own father by facilitating a bank robbery. The speed with which David agreed, though, surprised me . . . I tried to persuade him against the idea. But David thought it was brilliant . . . he would help arrange a situation in which my father and Hiram Canty would be assured of a successful robbery. David knew how deeply a robbery would hurt his prideful father. And he *wanted* to hurt him. I begged him not to cooperate with my father, not to carry out the scheme. He wouldn't listen.

"What David didn't know, what none of us knew, was that an innocent guard would be killed. Mr. Jericho's death devastated David . . . he wished afterward that he'd listened to me and not done it at all . . . I've never seen him so ruined as he was after that poor old guard died. And that was when I had an idea of my own, one that David agreed to right away."

"I think I can guess what you are about to tell me," I cut in. "You decided to get back as much of the stolen money as you could and give it to David to return to his father — to undo, as far as possible, what had been done."

"Yes . . . exactly. I urged him to do it, and even to try to reconcile with his father. It took David a long time to agree, and me a long time to actually get my hands on the money. But I did, or at least, a good part of it. I gave it to David in a blue carpetbag, and he got on that stagecoach to take the money back to his father, who was in Merritt that day, and confess and apologize for all he'd done."

"But your father and Canty realized what had happened, and intercepted and robbed the stagecoach to get the money back from David."

"Yes," she said. "And the result was all

this death . . . including David's. None of it should have happened. And if David had listened to me instead of to my father, it would *not* have happened. If only I could turn back the clock . . . I would find a way to persuade him."

"As I said already: don't fret over what can't be changed. The theologians say that not even God can change the past."

"But the price was so high . . . David is gone, forever."

"Yes. It is a high price. Far too high. But inescapable. Take heart, Miss Gavin. You were the voice of right, the voice of reason. The mistakes that were made were made by others, not you. If what you have told me is correct, you have nothing to regret, except the sorrow brought by the decisions of others who were less wise than you."

"Thank you, Mr. Wells . . . and thank you for caring about David and what happened to him."

"Miss Gavin, there is something I have to tell you: I know that Tate Barco is your father, but even so, I hope to see him punished for what he has done. I find I can't change that feeling even for your sake."

"I share the same sentiment, Mr. Wells. Remember: my own father killed the young man I loved, the young man I wanted to

132

spend my life with. I want to see him punished, too. He has been a father to me only in the most basic, physical sense. In all other senses, I have had no father, and no mother, really, except for my Aunt Anne."

"What if your father should be hanged, Merry? Would there be sadness for you?"

"Of course . . . he is my father, after all. But what evil comes to him, he has brought upon himself, as I said."

"Miss . . . there is nothing you can do to change the evil things that have happened, but there is a way you can see that justice is done. You can help the sheriff track down and arrest your father. You could do it for David . . . and for Mr. Jericho, and the driver and guard of that stagecoach."

"And for you, who took a bullet from my father's rifle."

"I am unimportant in this. My wound is minor and will heal. But by the way, in case it gives you any comfort, when your father fired the shot that struck David, I believe he was trying to shoot me instead. So he might not have planned to kill the young man."

"But did he seem regretful when he did?"

I could not lie. "No. He and Canty seemed to be happy about it."

"Because they saw David as a betrayer."

The sound of mournful voices carried to

my ears; another hymn being sung in the church down the street, heralding the close of the service. Time now for the burial.

What a somber day, dominated by death! One funeral concluding, David Flynn's about to commence. And somewhere, I supposed, the Freemans had also laid to rest Bailey Freeman . . . and what about Hiram Canty? Was there anyone alive to mourn a petty outlaw? Or — as seemed more likely — had he been laid to rest without ceremony in some pauper's hole out on public land somewhere, unmourned and with no one to drone dirges over his resting place? Would the partner who had killed him bother to visit his resting place? A carriage, quite a nice one, rolled down the street and parked a few yards away. It was driven by a very distinguished-looking black man with a mass of salt-and-pepper hair, and in the passenger area was Mrs. Estella Dupont. I politely parted from Merry and went over to extend an arm and help her down from the carriage.

"Mr. Wells . . . how good to see you!" she said. "I read the account in the newspaper . . . not a bad job, I thought."

"Yes . . . I think it was quite well done," I replied.

"I was shocked, though, to hear that you

were forced to defend the life of our sheriff against an assassin . . . but my praises to you for doing so! And sir . . . some thoughts I expressed on the stagecoach, regarding your persuasions during the late war . . . please accept my apology. Clearly I did not know at that point the kind of man you are, and would not have spoken as I did had I known."

"You needn't apologize . . . but if it will ease your mind for me to do so, I will accept," I told her.

"Oh . . . I see David's young woman over there. Mary."

"Merry Gavin . . . that's correct. I've been talking with her."

"She looks so sad!"

"She loved David very much, it seems. And she has other things in her life to make her sad."

"How tragic! Well, I think I shall enter and find myself a good place to sit."

"You should have your pick of seats at the moment."

I escorted her to the church and inside, where the coffin was just now being rolled to its place below the elevated pulpit. Mrs. Dupont wept a little when she saw it. And Albert Flynn came over and very politely greeted her. Her tears increased and she hugged him weeping onto his shoulder and telling him how well she understood his pain, having violently lost a son herself.

The banker clearly truly appreciated her presence and her words, and wept along with her, hugging her close. He would not look at me now — and that suited me fine. I'd had enough of Albert Flynn.

While Flynn was distracted, Merry Gavin took the opportunity to come inside. She sat down near the rear of the sanctuary, and in an attempt to make her more comfortable, I took a seat directly in front of her, blocking her, for the moment, at least, from being easily seen by Flynn. I hoped he would leave her alone now, especially as this would become an increasingly public place as more mourners arrived.

Noise outside. I rose and went to the front door. There I saw the great processional from the double funeral, a long line of people filing along slowly after the big hearse with its high-stepping horses. Among the mix was Charlie Crowder, who upon seeing me at the door cut out of the queue and in my direction. He trotted lightly up into the church.

"I be dogged if that wasn't the most mournful funeral I've ever been to!" he said. "It was one of them where the preacher thinks his job is to increase the misery of the bereaved ones. And he did his job, I can tell you that. What's going on here?"

"Another funeral . . . David Flynn's. Going to be a more high-brow affair than the one you just came from, I'd say."

"Yeah . . . you staying?"

"I might . . . but I'm much more conscious now of not being adequately dressed for a formal affair."

"I'd say old Albert Flynn will appreciate the thought, however you're dressed."

"I can't say I much care what Flynn appreciates or thinks."

"You met him?"

"Oh, yes. We had ourselves a conversation."

"I despise the arrogant old son of a gun myself . . . nose so high in the air he'd drown in a stout rain." Crowder looked back at the line of people still passing outside. "Oh, boy," he said sharply, under his breath. "Might want to get out of sight, Jed."

I was puzzled until I saw what had caught his eye. It was the gaggle of easily identifiable Freemans. They were together in the line, and three of them had spotted me and glared at me with an obvious hatred. The one farthest up stepped out of line and into a nearby alley, and the other two followed.

"They're going to lay for you, Jed," Charlie said. "They'll wait for you to come out, then they'll jump you, and next funeral I go to may be yours."

"You have a cheerful outlook," I said.

Maybe they'd grow tired of waiting, and move on. They didn't look like patient men.

At the moment, in the midst of this growing crowd and inside the walls of the church, I was probably safe from them. But I would be sure not to sit beside a window, just in case.

Merry Gavin rose and walked past me, heading into the foyer and from there into a small coatroom off its side. Another woman emerged as she entered, this woman smelling of fresh scented powder. Apparently the room was used not only for coats but as a primping room for women.

Merry had gone in there for emotional privacy. I could hear her crying, despite obvious efforts on her part to muffle her sobs. I felt badly for her . . . this was the funeral of a man she had probably hoped would be her husband. And the man had been killed by her own father.

Through the front door of the church walked Anne Stover, looking even lovelier than she had at the library. She saw me and nodded a greeting, which we returned, and then, ironically under the circumstances, she entered the cloakroom.

I had to smile. She'd just entered a room in which was a young woman she'd denied to me that she even knew. And there I was, outside the door, seeing her lie exposed with my own eyes. A clumsy situation for her. I heard her voice, speaking to Merry, giving her comfort. I was willing to bet she would not exit the room at the same time as Merry, though, and half a minute later I was proven right. Anne came out — alone, and this time would not meet my gaze. But she had to pass me as she entered the sanctuary, and as she did so I couldn't resist asking, "How is Miss Gavin?"

Anne Stover reddened; her eyes flicked over to me, then away again. "Very sad," she murmured, then got by me quickly, probably fearing I would confront her about her obvious earlier lie about Merry Gavin.

She found a seat on the west side of the sanctuary and sat stiffly, looking very uncomfortable. She kept glancing in my direction, apparently conscious I was watching her.

Merry eventually emerged from the coatroom and went into the sanctuary as well. She sat down beside Anne Stover, who suddenly looked even more uncomfortable and no longer glanced in my direction.

"Well, let's sit," Charlie said. We entered the sanctuary and sat on a back pew on the side of the church opposite Anne and Merry. More people entered, the sanctuary soon filling. Most of these were indeed from a different social stratum than the common folks who had dominated at the funeral of the stagecoach crewmen. This was a more blue-blooded, well-dressed crowd — many of them obviously the friends and relations of a banker, not a coachman. Yet there were also several people obviously not of means, not particularly well-dressed, and with calloused hands and the boots of working cattlemen or farmers.

"See these swells looking at us," Charlie whispered. "Looking at our clothes, these people are. Thinking how poorly dressed we are."

"I don't think so . . . I think they're thinking 'there's those two fellows who the paper wrote about,' " I replied. "They're probably thinking that we're a pair of heroes."

"Well, I really don't care either way about these high-climbers," he replied. "The higher a man climbs, the more ass he shows."

A woman seated in front of us heard this

comment and jumped as if she'd been stuck by a pin. She turned and looked at him as if he was sculpted from manure. Charlie grinned and winked at her and she turned forward again, quick as a pistol hammer snapping down.

10

At length the funeral began. An old organ in the corner played a hymn I had never heard . . . much more a classical-sounding piece of music than the standards that had been sung at the other funeral. Then a man with the pinched face worthy of a strict schoolmaster stood up with a black hymnal and began singing, his voice a warbling tenor that often drifted off its proper notes. This brought looks of fury from the young, long-haired organist, who was making several musical missteps of his own.

"Jed, if I should pass on, have them two do the music at my funeral, for that kind of caterwauling will surely raise the dead before this thing is through!" Charlie muttered to me. The woman in front of us spasmed again. Maybe the organist or vocalist was a relative.

The funeral dragged on, long, ceremonial, very formal. The priest presented a good but very stiff sermon, focusing as much on the evil of David's murderer as the tragedy of his loss. I watched Merry from the corner of my eye and wondered how difficult it was for her to listen to these things said about her own father, even if he wasn't a loved father.

The sermon showed no signs of moving toward an end. I leaned over to Charlie and whispered, very softly, "I've got to slip out of here and visit the outhouse."

"You can't do that!" he said. "You know who's out there, waiting for you!"

"It's been half an hour . . . they'll be gone by now. And the outhouse is on the opposite side of the church from where they hid. It's either go to the outhouse or pee out the window."

"I'll slip out, too," Charlie said, "and maybe I can keep an eye out for the Freeman clan."

We were both armed. We'd put on gun belts to come into town, for Repentance Creek had no ordinance against carrying pistols, and we were both deputies, anyway. Several other men in this place had guns as well, though most hid them beneath jackets in side holsters rather than wore gun belts. Ah, Texas! The frontier would live forever in this land, it seemed to me. I liked that.

Despite our efforts to be quiet, Charlie and I drew much attention as we left the church. I was glad to get out, not only for my suffering bladder's sake but also because the atmosphere inside was stifling in both a physical and mental sense. I vowed never to lie in state for a formal, overly ceremonial funeral. No, sir, I'd hop out of the coffin and flee the church in my dead man's shoes before I'd lie still for bilge like this.

We reached the outhouse without encountering any Freemans. I went in, and in fewer than twenty seconds, heard a gruff male voice, not Charlie's, outside. Then another, and then Charlie replied to whoever it was.

Charlie said, "No, sir, that's not who you think it is. My old pappy is in there . . . he's getting way up in years and he can't hold his water like he used to."

"That wasn't any old pappy I saw go in there," one of the voices answered. "The man who went in there is the one who killed Bailey . . . the one the newspaper thinks is so fine a hero!"

"You're wrong," Charlie said. "It's my pap in there."

"I know it's him because the man who shot Bailey is the same one Tate Barco wounded when he robbed that coach. And the man in there has his head wrapped in a cloth bandage."

I decided to wait inside a few minutes and hope that Charlie could talk them away from here.

He tried, perpetuating the story of "old pappy" in the privy, even calling in to "Pap" that he needn't hurry, because "these men out here are good and patient folks."

I gave out a loud, sickly sounding, old-mannish cough, in case they could hear me out there. Then I went to a knothole and peeked out. There they were, lingering at the edge of the woods, looking very frightening. The largest of them advanced toward Charlie, still in front of the outhouse.

"Hold on there, sir," Charlie said. "Pap will be out as quick as he can."

"We both know that ain't your father in there . . . and besides, I know who you are, Charlie Crowder!" said the big man. "Your pap lives in Arkansas!"

Charlie muttered something I couldn't understand, but the tone was fierce. This thing seemed to be building toward something explosive. And I decided I didn't want to be caught inside this little building when the explosion went off.

I went to the door and pushed out. The door bumped Charlie, who pushed back against the door and kept me trapped inside.

"Hey, Crowder, let him out!" one of the other yelled. "I think 'Pappy' is all through!"

Through the thin door I heard the unmistakable sound of Charlie's pistol being drawn from its holster. This was it: drawing his pistol would set them off if nothing else did. And sure enough, one of the Freemans — not the big one who was closest — fired a shot, maybe at Charlie, but maybe at me, because it came through the side wall, well above my head, and passed through and out the other side.

A wild shot, and I was lucky I'd not been hit by it. And I sure wouldn't linger inside waiting for the next bullet to come in lower. I put my shoulder to the door and rammed outward hard enough to counter Charlie's relatively meager weight.

I'd expected to encounter that weight when I shoved, but Charlie had picked the same moment to move, so when I hit the door full-force, there was nothing on the other side of it but open air. The door burst open wide and I staggered out like a drunken man, and ran straight into a human form. Not Charlie's, either, but the big Freeman who had been advancing on him. As we tumbled and fell together, I saw Charlie out of the corner of one eye. He was yards away, backing off, his pistol out and raised.

The other two Freemans came on in a rush, and Charlie fired. I heard a boyish yelp, and the apparent youngest of the Freemans staggered to the side and fell. The one beside him froze, then rushed to his side. He knelt and talked urgently to the boy, who kicked and jerked like injured horses do after they go down.

The big man with whom I'd entangled myself was a savvy fighter. He went after my most obvious weakness: my injured head. His fist struck me right on the bandaged area, creating a horrible jolt of pain that went through my entire skull, and also loosened the bandage. A second blow brought the bandage off completely; cloth fell down over my eyes, and I felt blood trickle around my left ear.

Charlie fired his pistol at my antagonist, but missed. It was enough to make the man get up and move, though. He shoved me away as if I weighed nothing, then stood on his massive feet. He stood astraddle of my prone form, and I thought about grabbing his thick legs and trying to trip him, but he would fall right atop me if I did so, and his weight would be of bone-crushing magnitude.

He stepped over me and rushed at Charlie. With him now not directly above me, I felt safe in grabbing for his right ankle and pulling back hard just as he attempted to take his next step. Unbalanced, he fell hard onto his face. Charlie raised his pistol and aimed it down at him. The man rolled over and looked up into the muzzle hole, which glared down at him like a black eye.

"Don't move an inch!" Charlie demanded.

The big man would naturally be expected to be cooperative with such a request in this situation, but he did the unexpected. His arms were as big around as Charlie's legs, and with his great strength he pushed up on the heels of his hands and very athletically pulled his feet forward at the same time, leaving him in a squatted posture on the ground in front of Charlie. Then a lunge up and forward, and he caught Charlie around the lower part of his chest and drove him to the ground. Enough of the man's weight hit Charlie's diaphragm to drive most of the wind out of his lungs. Worse, Charlie's hand struck a rock on the ground when he went down, and his pistol fell out of fingers gone numb from the impact.

The big man, whom I mentally tagged as "Crusher," clambered up on his victim, adding more weight and leaving Charlie even more helpless.

I raised my pistol. I was in a good position to shoot Crusher right in the groin, from below. But I couldn't make my finger pull the trigger. Part of it was sheer mercy: the thought of how horrific and painful a wound such a shot would be, in such a place and from such an angle, was too much even to think about. But the bigger part of what restrained me was the realization of how much death I'd already been involved with since coming to Texas, and my urgent wish not to be involved in more. So I lay there in an awkward, twisted posture on the ground, aiming at the bulky man who was crushing the air out of Charlie, while the second Freeman continued tending the one Charlie had shot.

If I couldn't shoot to kill, I could surely shoot to wound, and maybe put him out of action. So I aimed along the side of his big rump and firing a shot that plowed through the outer side of his left buttock, digging under the skin and plowing a tunnel before emerging just below hip level. His whole body drew up at the impact of the bullet and he let out a low, long moan. Blood began to soak visibly through his trousers.

Noise behind me made me roll. The gunfire had drawn attention from the church where the funeral was still in progress, and now men were emerging and coming our way, drawing pistols from beneath their Sunday-best dress coats.

I got up, aware suddenly of how much blood was coming from my re-injured head wound. "Look . . . Wells is shot again!" one of the new arrivals yelled. "Who did it?"

"He ain't shot again!" yelled back the second Freeman, the one tending to the wounded one. "Ain't nobody shot him . . . but Crowder shot my baby brother! And now Wells has shot my cousin in the fundament!"

"Crusher," as I mentally labeled the one who'd come after Charlie, got up and managed to stay up in spite of his wounded rump. He staggered over and kicked me, which made me mad and caused me to leap up and drive my fist into his jaw. He grunted and fell against the outhouse, literally rocking it. The door was still open, and when he lost his footing a moment later, he fell inside the little structure, hitting his head on the side of the seat.

I went in, literally walking on his body to get inside. Once in, I stepped off him on to the outhouse floor, leaned over, and grabbed his collar with my right hand, his hair with my left. He was stunned, but still conscious. With a great exertion I pulled up on his collar and hair and managed to haul his head over to the hole in the seat. I jammed his face into the hole and pushed down. His head squeezed slowly through, almost all the way . . . and then plunged through completely. The hole was large enough that it accommodated his neck with some room to spare, but not enough to let him get his head back out again without peeling off his ears.

One of the men from the funeral appeared in the door and took in the situation. "Well, precious, how's the smell down there?" he asked Crusher, laughing.

Crusher bellowed cursewords at the foulness he was forced to observe and smell below him, but they were muffled. I stepped out of the outhouse and was suddenly hit by something large. I fell onto my right side and the thing that had hit me — Freeman number two — comforter of the wounded one — landed on top of me.

I'd had enough of this kind of thing. Angry, I pushed him off and got up. He got up as well, so I hit him on the jaw, knocking him down again. He bounded up once more while a crowd fresh from the Flynn funeral began to gather around us. I took the next blow, which shivered my jaw and left me dizzy. But I held together well enough to react effectively, sending several repeated blows into the jaws of my opponent. He fought back, and our little dance worked its way around the back of the outhouse. I could hear Crusher still cursing and thumping about inside. He was trying to get his head out, but it would stay stuck where it was until somebody rounded up a can of axle grease.

Busy as I was, I noticed something about the structure of the outhouse. The back side of it suffered greatly from rot, so that the boards that extended below floor level were decayed away, leaving the rear edge of the pit exposed. An inspiration came. I redoubled my efforts and landed a particularly hard punch on my foe's chin. He fell down and back, his head and shoulders in the direction of the outhouse.

I ran up, grabbed his feet, and shoved his prone body toward the edge of the pit. He grasped what I was trying to do at the final moment, and grabbed hold of the wall as the back of his head cleared the edge of the pit. But I shoved harder than he could hold, and his body slid further in. No doubt he and Crusher looked at each other eye-to-eye for a moment or two. Then his body tilted down, and his own weight pulled him down in a backward, headfirst dive. When he hit below the noise was a combination of a splash and a splat. He screamed and thrashed around. Foul material splattered out of the hole, some of it going high enough to spot the down-looking face of Crusher, who had the best view of all of what had happened to his companion.

"Whoa!" Charlie Crowder yelled as I turned around. He had a big smile on his face, admiration in his eyes, and my pistol in his hand. Apparently I'd lost it in the commotion. "Now, that's where to dump a piece of dung!" he said. "Congratulations, Jed Wells! No wonder you're a writer — talk about an imaginative solution to a problem!"

"We've still got one free, though," I said. "Although admittedly, he is wounded, thanks to your marksmanship, Charlie."

"Let's dump him in the hole, too."

"How about let's get the local law involved and let them handle it."

"We are the local law . . . we're deputized!"

"We're county, not town . . . this is inside the town. Is there not a town marshal?"

"Right here," a skinny man with pale blond hair said, coming around the outhouse. "Morrison East," he said, sticking out his hand, which I shook. "I'm marshal of the town of Repentance Creek."

"I'm Jed Wells, writer, visitor to town . . . and believe it or not, temporary deputy for Rabun County, Texas."

East was dressed nicely; apparently he'd been an attender of the funeral, too. "Well, you've done quite a job of rounding up the varmits here today, deputy. I never seen an outhouse put to so appropriate a use."

"You know the Freeman family, I take it."

"Oh, yes, I know them well, as does Sheriff Strickland, every Texas Ranger who ever passed through this county, and just about anybody else you can name. Hey, you're the one who killed Bailey Freeman, aren't you!"

" 'Fraid so."

"Too bad you didn't get the rest of the clan."

"Well, leave that one with his head stuck in that hole and he'll eventually die of breathing in the bad air. Leave the other down in the pit and he'll finally lose strength and collapse and drown or suffocate. And the youngest one is wounded — Charlie shot him — a justified shooting, and Charlie's a deputy too, if that matters."

"Let's get this mess cleaned up," the marshal said. "And let's wash these Freemans off before we lock 'em up. Otherwise,

I'll not be able to endure the smell."

A saw was required to free Crusher from his unusual trap. After that, the outhouse was pushed over on its side and the victim in the pit was pulled out. By then Charlie and I had worked our way off the scene and were walking down a side street and hoping to get away from any other Freemans who might be roaming around. But someone did follow. I heard a familiar scritch-scratch sound, wheeled, and saw Pembrook Jones. He was scribbling on his pad so intently he almost walked right into me.

"Mr. Jones, don't tell me you witnessed our latest adventure as well!"

"I was in the church for the funeral and came out when I heard the shooting," he said. "I must say I've never seen troublesome men dealt with in such an unusual, and in their case appropriate, fashion."

"Are Charlie and I to grace the pages of the newspaper again?"

"Were you unhappy with my earlier reporting?"

I thought about my answer. "Not unhappy, no. You were surprisingly detailed and accurate. But such things are not what I wish to be known for. Too much of this, and my publishing house may have something to say to me. The founder of Gage

House lives in this county, you know."

"Is it Mr. Gage the rancher?"

"Yes . . . the very man I came to Texas to see. I didn't come to be robbed, or to shoot at wife-beating assassins or stagecoach robbers, or to dispose of troublesome locals in outhouse pits. I simply wanted to meet with Mr. Gage and recruit his support for a novel I want to write."

"And I'm simply trying to cover the news of this county, Mr. Wells."

"I know . . . but can we let this one pass? I have enough bad will with the Freeman family already. A newspaper story will only make it worse."

"All this happened outside a church where the son of the county's biggest banker was being memorialized," he said. "It was witnessed by dozens . . . I can't ignore it and hope to retain any reputation as a dedicated newspaperman."

"I suppose not. Just keep it as restrained as you can, please."

"Of course."

11

He asked me a few questions and I answered them as best I could. Then I had one for him. "The funeral . . . did the disturbance end it?"

"No, it was continuing when I went outside . . . just with a lot fewer still in attendance. The shooting drew out most of the men . . . especially those carrying guns."

"Where will the burial be?"

"A private plot, edge of town. Near the bank, in fact."

"Let's head that way," I said to Charlie.

He nodded and we walked back to the nearest street, Jones accompanying us.

"Which way?" I asked at the end of the street.

Both pointed north. We headed that way, Jones still finding something to scribble on his pad. The man apparently never quit working.

The burial service was under way, the

warbling tenor rendering another tune. No organ to accompany him this time, so he got off key even more frequently. Charlie reminded me of my bloodied condition, and we paused at a watering trough, where I cleaned up as best I could despite the unsanitary state of the water.

I'd come not for the service but for Anne Stover and Merry Gavin. I saw the two of them standing together at the rear of the crowd, their backs toward us. I glanced at Charlie, who signaled for us to keep silent, and we walked slowly over to stand a few yards behind them. The newspaperman, still with us, looked over the assembly and jotted more notes.

When it was over and the final prayer said, Anne turned and saw Charlie and I standing there. Her eye fixed on mine and this time she didn't look away. Merry saw Charlie and me as well, and smiled, probably unaware that her aunt at her side had denied knowing her when we visited at the library.

"Mrs. Stover," I said.

She looked at my now-exposed, wounded head. "I hope the sight of me isn't too shocking," I said. "I regret the loss of the bandage, and will replace it."

"I am not shocked," she said. "Just sorry

for you that you must endure the discomfort."

"I'm doing well with it," I told her. "In fact, I think having no bandage on is makes me feel better." I looked at Merry. "Miss Gavin," I said, "I am pleased to see you again, though I remain dreadfully sorry about the circumstances."

"Thank you for your sympathies, Mr. Wells."

Anne looked uncomfortable indeed, and I rather meanly made it worse for her by saying, "I'm told you work at the library with your aunt, Miss Gavin?"

"I do," she said. "I love books . . . I've always loved books. So did David."

"Might I have a private word with you at your convenience, Mr. Wells?" Anne Stover asked me.

"Of course." We stepped off a few paces, and she surprised me by taking my arm. "Mr. Wells, I owe you an apology for having been less than forthright with you earlier on."

"Regarding your niece, you mean."

"Yes. I probably should not have lied to you. But I didn't know what might come of your inquiries, and I would not for any cause bring upon that child more trouble than she has already had in life. And there

159

are things not everyone knows . . . and that is how it should be."

"I don't fault your intentions," I told her. "I probably would have done the same in your place. But now that I have learned the truth from other sources, may we speak more candidly than before?"

"Indeed, sir . . . but first tell me what the 'truth' is that you have learned."

"That Miss Gavin is the daughter of Tate Barco, a connection through your late husband's family. That you, by marriage, are her aunt . . . and were greatly involved in her raising. That she indeed does work with you at the library. And that she, I am sorry to say, is greatly despised by Albert Flynn, who seems to hold against her that her father is an outlaw who has plagued him."

"And plagued him now worse than ever through the murder of poor David."

"Yes. So tell me: are these things I've been told all true?"

She nodded sadly.

"I had the opportunity to talk to Miss Gavin prior to David's funeral," I said. "I had also spoken by then to Albert Flynn . . . the conversation in that case being less than a pleasure."

"Indeed. He despises me deeply, and my

feelings toward him are hardly better. He made his son's life a misery."

"He admitted to me that they were quite at odds. He struck me as a man whom it would be difficult to have as a father."

"Indeed."

"Let me ask you, Anne — may I call you Anne? — is it generally known that Merry is the daughter of Tate Barco?"

"No, no . . . it is known by very few, and I seek for Merry's sake to keep that relationship little known. But Flynn knows."

"I'm surprised he has not spread the information out of sheer meanness."

"I think what has restrained him is that fact that she and David were known to be in love. Could a man of his pride bear to have it known that his own son was involved with the daughter of an infamous outlaw?"

"I suppose not. Anne, I have a question: how has Barco managed to live so infamously and be known by so many, yet remain free? Why has the sheriff not been able to capture him?"

"Tate is slippery and clever . . . and there are plenty who do not like the stagelines, the railroads, or the banks — particularly given Albert Flynn's arrogance and contempt for the common folk — and they protect him at times."

161

"That surprises me to a degree . . . clearly his actions during the stage robbery, and the fact he killed an elderly guard at the bank, shows that he holds no regard for people of any station. How could he gain the public sympathy?"

"You must understand that Tate did not practice his criminality in this region until recently. He had robbed banks in Kansas, Missouri, and Illinois before he came here, but those crimes had no local impact and no one was particularly interested in seeing him caught. And realize as well that his success at crimes elsewhere had left him with money . . . and for all his flaws, Tate Barco can be generous. He has shared his wealth with people who needed help badly, and he gained some good favor with the public. People are always ready to love outlaws, for some reason. And Tate knows how to play off that. But his good favor is fading fast . . . ever since the bank robbery and Mr. Jericho's death. I've heard so much talk among people at the library and on the street . . . he's a hated man now, and I can assure you that since the killings during the stage robbery, he's hated all the more."

"Remarkable!" I said. "Another question: I know how people perceive Albert Flynn . . . but how did they perceive David?

162

Was he seen as 'uppity' like his father, or one of the common folk?"

"He was young and not known as well as his father, but he did help manage the bank, and he'd gained many friends through his kindness and cordiality . . . everything his father was not. He was empowered to give loans, and would do so for those who needed them badly . . . people were beginning to go to him and avoid Albert altogether . . . whether Albert noticed, I don't know. If he did, he probably resented David for it . . . either that or he felt glad to be bothered by fewer people below his station."

"You really have no regard for him, do you?"

"As much as he has for me."

"If you should see Tate . . . if he should seek your protection from the law . . . would you give it to him?"

"At one time, maybe. Not now. Not after David."

"What about Merry?"

"Merry would never help him now, not since he took the life of the man she loved so much. I believe that at this point, she'd pull the lever on the gallows trapdoor with her own hands, if asked to do so."

"Do you know, or would Merry know, where Tate Barco could likely be found?"

"No . . . no . . . he had always kept his hiding places secret. I suspect there is a woman somewhere he stays with from time to time, but I don't know. Oddly, as evil as he is, he is a man with a Puritanical streak about some things . . . he may commit certain sins, but he will not flaunt them."

"A strange man."

"An evil man. Never to be trusted."

"But your husband's sister must have loved him."

"My husband was not an intelligent man . . . nor was his sister."

"He must have had some intelligence, given who he married."

She lifted a brow and smiled. "What a kind thing to say."

"I've written many better lines than that one."

"I intend to become a serious reader of your work."

"I hope you will enjoy it. Have you read none of it before now?"

"I've seen the books, scanned some pages. Grim subjects . . . I think it put me off of them some."

"They are grim at times . . . but there is something worthwhile in them, I like to think."

"I will read them. I promise."

We talked a while longer, then Charlie meandered our way. Anne smiled at him, and to my private displeasure she seemed quite interested in talking to him. I felt rejected and wandered off alone, tired of this county, tired of Texas, tired of worry, tired of being known by everyone I ran across because of a situation I'd as soon not have been involved in at all.

I vowed to find and talk to Walter Gage at my first opportunity, then leave Texas behind and get back to the life I knew. Tate Barco could be hanged, and alongside him, for all I'd allow myself to care, they could string up Charlie Crowder, Anne Stover, Merry Gavin, and everybody else I'd met since I got here.

The night was spent on a small but comfortable bed in a small room in Jim Clelland's ranch house. Crowder opted for a blanket spread out in a loft at the stable. No doubt I was more comfortable, but sleep did not want to come to me.

It was something Charlie had told me after we returned from Repentance Creek. He'd talked to Anne Stover for a long time and discovered she provided good companionship. She'd even let him walk her over to the library, which she'd closed for the funerals, and issued to him an invitation to visit her home the next evening for supper, which she would cook. Did fried chicken suit him?

He'd informed me that he'd not forgotten me, and had managed to wrangle an invitation for me as well.

It wasn't flattering to know I was a last-minute add-on . . . and even then only because Charlie Crowder had insisted on it.

God help me, I was actually jealous.

Going loco, it seemed. Just one more reason to get out of this place as quickly as I could.

I got out of my bed and went to the window of my little room. The sun spilled across the beautiful landscape. I scanned it, studying the horizon and trying to imagine everything that lay beyond it, as far as a man could go . . . and then I saw a buggy approaching the house, coming up the long dirt road, pulled by a strong-pacing chestnut horse. Who could be coming here first thing in the morning? Maybe the sheriff, though I didn't think of him as the buggy-driving kind.

Pancho was up and about his work, probably had been since before sunrise. From somewhere in the house a wonderful breakfast smell arose. God bless Rosalita and

166

good women like her everywhere! Pancho was a fortunate man, and I wondered if he knew it.

The buggy was quite close now, Pancho walking out to meet it. I looked closely, squinting, and recognized the driver. It was quite a surprise.

I'd brought a pitcher full of water to my room the night before, and poured some of it into a wash basin. As best I could I quickly washed up; shaving would have to come later. Dressing and combing my hair, I left my room and headed downstairs and out the door.

Clelland was already striding across toward the buggy, which was passing through the big gate at the edge of the yard. He was reaching up and shaking hands with the driver when I got there.

"Good morning, Walter," I said. "You're looking good these days."

"Jed!" Walter Gage said, still pumping Clelland's hand. "Good to see you. I'd tell you that you were looking good, too, but that wound on your head would make a liar out of me. I read about what happened in the paper. Are you all right?"

"Quite fine," I said. "Quite fine, thanks largely to Mr. Clelland's hospitality."

"Excellent!" Walter said. He finally quit

shaking Clelland's hand, and to him said, "You know, Jim, your guest here is one of the finest writers ever published by the publishing house I founded. I'm proud to have played a role in getting his career started."

"Well, you know books better than most," Clelland said. "Maybe someday we'll have you understanding the cattle business, too."

"Don't hold your breath on that one, Jim," Gage said. Then he studied me up and down. "I believe you're thinner than the last time I saw you, Jed."

"It's living on the road, Walter. Wears a man down. Here to there and back again, then back the other way one more time."

"Well, I'm glad your 'here' or 'there' included a stop in Rabun County. I knew from your letter that you were coming . . . but I didn't expect to learn of your arrival by reading of violent heroics in the local newspaper."

"It wasn't in the plan, Walter."

"How's the head? I read you suffered a plowing."

"I'll make it. Rosalita, Pancho's woman, has doctored me quite well."

"No bandage?"

"Lost it. But I'm better without it. And I've realized that I can comb my hair in just

168

a certain way and hide it. So, Walter, tell us about the cattleman's life."

"I can't . . . haven't lived enough of it yet. I'm still learning."

"But slowly . . . he's learning slowly," Clelland said. "Without the guidance of wise old experts like me, this man would be building cow coops in his backyard and lifting up his cows to look for eggs every morning."

"Don't listen to him," Gage said. "I'm not nearly so helpless nor hopeless as that. The man loves exaggeration."

"Come inside, Walter," Clelland said. "There's still coffee, and food."

Indeed there was. Mexican though she was, the breakfast Rosalita had cooked was pure Southern America — eggs, ham, biscuits, even a big dishful of grits, laden with butter. Clelland had had a good influence on this woman. We all dined with utter satisfaction.

Finished at last, we rose and headed for the nearest comfortable chairs. Rosalita eyed me and I could tell she was waiting to see if I would help her with the dishes again.

Not this time, Rosalita. This was my opportunity to talk to the man I'd come to Texas to see. He and I headed for the porch, seeking a little privacy. Gage settled into one rocking chair and I into another . . . and Charlie Crowder came out and sat on the porch rail, propped up against a post. I didn't mind . . . Charlie was not an intrusive presence. Gage and I could still talk.

"So you've got an idea for your next book, Jed?" he asked.

"Yes," I told him. "It springs off my last one . . . but looking at the time before that story, not after."

"Interesting. Tell me more."

I did the best I could, telling my story with all the energy a man stuffed with breakfast could muster. Leaning toward him, I let the full intensity of my conviction flame upon him. I *would* sell him on my idea, if it could be done.

Gage was a man hard to read, and I couldn't tell how much I was reaching him. At last my efforts ended; I had said all I could say. I drew in a long breath, looked at Gage's expressionless face, and said, "Well?"

"An excellent idea, Jed. No doubt one you would carry off well. But it is not the story you should write. Not at all."

"Then what is?" I asked, making no effort to hide my disappointment.

"The story you are living, right here in Rabun County," he said.

"Amen," muttered Charlie Crowder.

"What . . . all this with the stagecoach robber, and Barco, and all that?"

"Yes indeed . . . what a story, Jed! What a story! You must write it! If you do, I assure you, you will have a book on your hands that this entire nation will not be able to put down."

"I don't want to write this," I said. "I don't even want to live it."

"Now, Jed . . . some maturity here, my friend! You are not a boy, but a man . . . make the decision of wisdom and age, not some impassioned boyish impulsiveness."

"You just said you liked my idea . . . why not let me write it?"

"Why settle for a pewter spoon when you have a setting of fine silver at hand?" Gage asked. "You are living out a thrilling, chilling adventure . . . don't let this opportunity pass, Jed."

"So you won't support what I want to do? My idea is a 'pewter spoon' to you?"

"I will support what it is *best* for you to do." He paused and grinned. "You've not done poorly by listening to me in the past, son. Don't turn a deaf ear to me now."

"I'll listen, Walter. You know I always do."

"Yes . . . yes." He leaned back, looking satisfied, then spoke to Charlie. "I'm glad your friend here has the wisdom to respect the wisdom of an old man," he said. "I thought for a moment there that the only satisfaction this day was going to bring me was the fine breakfast we enjoyed this morning, and the pleasant, lovely company I will enjoy tonight."

" 'Lovely company?' Walter . . . have you a lady friend?"

"No, no, not an old dog like me. But apparently my company is desirable for some of the fair sex . . . I've been invited to dine this evening at the home of the lovely librarian of Repentance Creek . . . a beautiful, intelligent, gracious woman you should meet, Jed."

"I've met her. Anne Stover is a delightful beauty. But I'm obliged to tell you, Walter: you'll not be the only person fortunate enough to share her company and dine at her table tonight."

"That's right," said Charlie. "She set up this little dinner party just as a way of getting *me* over to her house. That pretty little heifer's got her eye set on me so hard I don't think I'll be able to keep my precious freedom for long."

Walter stared at his feet. "I guess I was an old fool indeed to believe she would find the prospect of an evening's conversation with an old man, all by himself, to be appealing. I see now I'm only an item of lesser interest. Window dressing, as they say."

"I rather doubt that, Walter," I said. "Given your history with the library, your publishing background, and your general love of books, I'm sure she finds you a fascinating man."

"But it's *me* who has her heart in my pocket," Charlie said. "You bookish swells need to remember that."

"You live in a world of great dreams, my friend," I told Charlie.

He gave a cocky grin, left the porch, and headed for the outhouse around back. Clelland leaned back, propped his boot heels on the rail of the porch, and began to snore. Walter Gage and I went back to talking books, and before I knew it I had agreed to consider strongly his proposal that I base my next work on my current adventures. Still, I maintained my arguments against it. "The truth is, Walter, none of this is anything I have a natural inclination to write about," I told him. "I didn't come to Texas to do these things, and I don't want to turn the death of innocent people into something I profit from."

"You've written about the deaths of innocent people through all your work so far, Jed. You're not exploiting them . . . only the circumstances, that's all. And there is a great difference between exploiting people and exploiting circumstances."

"Well, I hope my circumstances will be more peaceful and much less exploitable from now on. I'm eager to have adventures behind me."

"Well, indeed you are a public enough figure that your exploits on the stagecoach and your shooting of that assassin may easily find their way into a major newspaper somewhere. They pick up things from little local journals like the ADVOCATE, you know. And you're right: that sort of publicity may not seem ideal — but do remember that your actions are seen on almost all sides as heroic! So perhaps it is better publicity than we think, eh?"

Clelland shifted in his seat and his right foot lost its perch on the rail. His heel slammed down hard on the porch and he jerked awake. "Whaaa!" he yelled.

Rosalita came to the door. "Sir . . . what is wrong?" she asked him.

"Nothing . . . nothing . . . I just need more coffee. And some for Jed and Walter, as well, please, Rosalita."

Charlie Crowder came back around the house. "And for Mr. Crowder as well?"

174

Rosalita asked.

"Mr. Crowder *what* as well?" said Charlie. "More coffee?"

"Lord no . . . any more coffee and I'll be living the rest of the day in that privy," he said. "*Gracias* anyway, Mrs. Valdez."

12

Walter Gage did not leave, but visited for hours with Clelland, talking cattle and markets and the like. Despite the prevailing tendency on all sides to treat Walter as a hopelessly neophyte rancher, it was clear he had a better grasp of his new way of life than even he was prone to admit. I was impressed by my old mentor's versatility.

But I didn't hear much of what he said. Charlie and I threw in with Pancho and other ranch hands, and I laid aside the career of writer and part-time volunteer deputy to enjoy instead a day of vigorous exercise, sunshine, and fresh air, helping out around the ranch. Refreshing work for a man whose labors usually were done at a table inside a shadowed little room.

"You taking your fancy buggy to that dinner party tonight?" Clelland asked Gage at the close of a fine luncheon served by Rosalita in early afternoon. As guests, we'd eaten not with the rest of the hands at the bunk-house dining hall, but at Clelland's table, and had returned to relax on the porch afterward. Two big meals within the span of a few hours was almost more than I could handle, and even rail-thin Charlie looked a little stuffed and stretched around the middle, this despite the physical labor we'd done since breakfast.

"I suppose I'll take the buggy," he said. "But I'll have to drive it home in a little while so I can change into suitable attire for the evening."

"Well, Walter, I'll make you a deal. You and I are about the same size," Clelland said. "I've got three new suits — *three* of them — and if you'll stay here today, you're welcome to one of them. And you can give Jed and Charlie a stylish ride in that pretty vehicle."

"Have you anything in gray?"

"I do. Consider it yours."

"Are you not coming yourself to Mrs. Stover's dinner, Jim?" Gage asked.

"No," Clelland replied, sounding sour. "I've not been invited. Too bad for me! Anne is excellent company for any man. Refreshment for the soul and the masculine eye. Her associate Merry is just the same."

"Yes, indeed."

I admit I was a little disheartened to learn that tonight's gathering was such a large affair. Still, it was something I expected to enjoy, unless it proved to be too residually tainted by the funeral atmosphere of the prior day. I for one was ready to forget about death and sorrow for a while.

The group on the porch eventually broke apart, people heading in different directions to pursue different tasks. Only Gage and I remained, talking books. He pressed the case for using these Texas experiences as grist for the next book, and his case, I had to admit, was strong. Adding strength to it was the practical consideration that Gage would throw his influence much more strongly behind a book whose creation he had urged rather than one more or less forced upon him by a stubborn author.

As the afternoon wore on, my resistance to his arguments wore down, and despite some inner reluctance was already making mental outlines of the story I would tell. Meanwhile, I worked, helping Charlie expand a corral and then starting the construction of a storage shed. The day passed quickly, and as the sun began to wester, Clelland called us away from labor. Time to clean up and dress . . . an evening in the company of the lovely Anne Stover was at hand.

The house of Anne Stover surprised me. Not by its neatness, the beauty of the aromatic flowers growing around its porch, or the taste with which it was decorated, because I had expected all those things. What surprised me was the house's size. It was a two-story, gingerbread-trimmed dwelling, painted the color of sand, the curtains in its large windows a muted red, the interior walls papered in a floral pattern.

Merry Gavin's dwelling was much smaller and much more simply made . . . a clapboarded rectangle with a small porch and yard that blended into the yard of Anne's house. The effect of the two houses together was appropriately symbolic: Anne's house seemed to loom over and protect that of her neice. I wondered why they simply hadn't moved Merry into Anne's house. Perhaps Anne hadn't wanted to lose all her privacy.

The evening brought wonderful revelations of what miracles could be performed with a frying chicken and a skillet. Anne served the finest fried chicken I'd tasted since leaving my old Kentucky homeplace . . . batted with a crust of bread crumbs, cooked to perfect tenderness, served with marvelous vegetables and butter-drenched biscuits so light they almost floated, the meal had every man there dreaming of marrying Anne Stover. Could there be a more perfect woman than she?

But those of us who were actually of an age that marriage to Anne would be conceivable suffered a bruising of pride. Anne's attentions were paid this evening almost entirely to gray-haired Walter Gage. Literature, arts, and the need to improve the status of both in this little town dominated Anne's mind. Merry, perched beautifully on her chair at the north corner of the table, contributed intelligently to the conversation, and I, as a writer, had some worthwhile things to say as well. Poor Charlie, who read mostly dime novels, newspapers, and the biblical Book of Proverbs, was left with little to contribute to the conversation. Despite his earlier silly braggadocio about possessing the heart of the lovely Anne, and the way he'd lorded over me the fact that he had been the one to wrangle an invitation for me to this affair, I felt sorry for him. He was a good man, and I could not fault him for being smitten by so lovely a woman.

Walter enjoyed his role as guest of honor, and played it masterfully. He began a discussion of British satire that could not have been bettered, I believed, in the finest classrooms of Oxford. The man was brilliant. Just today he'd sat and talked with a grizzled old cattleman and now he was just as proficiently discussing literature with an intelligent and well-read librarian.

Anne, equally intrigued by my old mentor, eventually called Walter upstairs to her personal library to examine some old and rare European books she believed might be of significant value. Gage, among his other talents, was an excellent appraiser of books and antiquities related to them.

As the pair of them headed up the stairs, Charlie cast a baleful gaze in their direction, then rolled it around to me. "Ah, me!" he said. "I guess the Lord humbles the prideful."

"What do you mean, Mr. Crowder?" asked Merry, who had been sitting so silently that we'd almost forgotten her presence. I actually started at the sound of her voice.

Charlie had forgotten her as well, or else he never would have started a conversation with such an undertone. He looked blankly at Merry, then smiled. "Oh, nothing . . . just an old cowboy's chatter," he said. "I guess I'm ashamed to be so ignorant compared to such as Mr. Gage and your aunt."

"You're hardly ignorant, sir," she said. "I've heard it said that there is no one in the county who knows cattle better than you."

He grinned broadly. "Obviously you have been talking to people of notable wisdom."

I gave Charlie a grin. I knew what he'd really meant about having his pride humbled. If he'd been asked earlier in the day who would be most likely to climb the stairs with Anne Stover, he would have claimed that status for himself . . . and it wouldn't be to examine a bunch of old books that he'd make that upstairs journey. I knew what he was thinking even if Merry Gavin didn't . . . though I suspected that maybe she knew more than she let on.

Merry didn't linger, declaring herself tired from her day and still wearied by grief, she departed the house and headed to her own residence. Charlie and I were left alone downstairs.

"You and me, partner," he said. "And all the fair ladies have fled."

"You're telling my life story," I replied.

"You know, I was just joshing around today, talking big about her inviting me here because she had notions about me . . . but the truth is, I was trying to persuade myself that just maybe, maybe . . . but I can tell from listening to her talk tonight that she's never going to be interested in a man like me. She needs a smart man, like Gage is."

"Walter Gage could be her father, old as he is. Maybe her grandfather. She's not interested in him, Charlie."

"Lord, man, I know that! That's not what I'm saying. I'm saying that the man she does take an interest in will have to be like Gage . . . intelligent, educated, all wrapped up in books and such." He paused. "A man like you, for example."

I weighed that notion, then nodded. "I'd have little to complain about if such a woman ever took a shine to me, Charlie. I won't deny that. But I don't have any cause to believe such is the case."

"I know what you mean, friend."

Just then, we heard a scream from upstairs . . . Anne's scream, muffled slightly by walls and floors. Charlie and I stared at each other, eyes big as coffee cup rims, then came to our feet simultaneously.

"What is that old bastard trying up there?" Charlie asked. "I didn't think that old duck would have that in him!"

I still couldn't believe he had it in him . . . surely it was something besides Walter that had made her scream.

She screamed again as Charlie and I reached the top of the stairs. We followed the sound down the short hallway and through an open door to the right. The room was lined with shelves and filled with books. Anne Stover and Walter Gage were at the side window, looking out and down . . . in the direction of Merry's house.

They glanced at us as we entered, but that was all. Whatever held their attention was apparently of extraordinary interest.

"What's wrong, Walter?" I asked.

He looked at me, very troubled. "A problem over at Merry's house," he said.

"A peeper," Anne said.

"What?"

"Someone at her back window."

Charlie and I froze for a moment, then moved as one, back into the hall, down the stairs, out the door. He circled right, a more direct route to the place the offender was, and I went around the front of the house to intercept him if he ran away from Charlie.

Charlie got to him first, and it was like an explosion: flesh colliding with flesh, two grunting masculine yells, and the sound of falling bodies. I rounded the back of the house in time to see Charlie scrambling to his feet and his opponent doing his best to get away. I could make things out only because of light coming from the window. When the runner reached me, I was shocked by how young he was . . . hardly more than a boy. Young or not, he'd done a thing that couldn't be abided. I reached out and snared him by the shoulder with my left hand, then sent my right smacking into his left jaw. He staggered backward on his heels, fell on his rump.

Then the light inside went dark and I could not see him at all for a moment, until my eyes adjusted to the dim moonlight.

The land behind the two houses rose fairly sharply — quite a hill, really, for these flat parts — and the young offender was scrambling up it as fast as he could. I went after him, but Charlie was ahead of me, and got to him before he reached the hilltop. I got there in time to be bowled over as the young man struggled and pulled and broke out of Charlie's grasp, his body thumping hard against me, knocking me back down. I almost rolled down the hill, but managed to get a double handhold in the wild grass and stopped myself. Twisting about, I glimpsed Charlie chasing the young man over the crest of the hill. I got up and went after them.

They were fighting again when I found them next. The moonlight seemed brighter on the far side of the hill, and though I could not see them clearly, I could tell generally what was happening. Fists flew, and occasionally there was the thudding slap of a blow connecting. Mostly, though, they seemed to be flailing, fighting in the dark and often missing one another. I drifted in close, looking for a chance to intervene on Charlie's behalf, but a wild blow struck me on the injured side of my head, and I went down in a burst of blue and red stars.

I lost awareness of everything for a time, then opened my eyes and found myself in a new place, with new company. An old fellow with white locks and drooping jowls walked past the place where I lay. He had a broom in hand and a dirty apron across his broad body. He looked over at me and raised high two very thick eyebrows when he saw me looking back at him. Turning, he hurried out of the room, which was as strange and unknown to me as he was.

He was back a moment later, followed by a younger man in a white coat. The latter man came to my bedside, pulled up a chair, and sat down. The old man began sweeping in the far corner of the room.

"I'm Dr. Greaves," he said. "I'm glad to

see you conscious again, Mr. Wells."

It all came back and I sat up. "Where is Charlie? Did he get the boy?"

"There was a kidnapping," the doctor said. "That's what I was told by the sheriff, in any case."

The sheriff? He'd been nowhere around when the incident at Merry's house occurred. If he'd been called in, signficant time must have passed.

"Who was kidnapped?" I asked.

"The young woman who lived in the house, I think."

"Merry Gavin?"

"That is correct."

"Dear God! Who kidnapped her?"

"There was a gang of men there, hiding behind the house. One of their number — a young man — went to the window of the house to make sure the victim was present, and then, as the sheriff passed it on to me, you and the other man intervened. You apparently suffered a blow to the head, which in combination with your prior wound was sufficient to knock you unconscious. Meanwhile, the others of the gang joined the first one in battling with the other gentleman with you, and he too was knocked senseless. Then the gang invaded the young woman's home and spirited her away. An apparent kidnapping." He paused. "She is a beautiful young lady . . . we may hope for her sake that the motives for the capture were not carnal."

I felt sick. Merry . . . suffering kidnap and God only knew what else. So what had appeared to be a mere incident of a young man trying to watch a pretty girl in her home obviously had been much more. He was merely the point of the arrow — probably the youngest and least important of the gang, and thus the one sent down for the initial and dangerous look for the victim.

The doctor's theory that Merry might have been kidnapped for carnal use was plausible, but given all that had happened in the last two days, my guess was there was more to it than that. This kidnapping surely related to all that had gone on.

But who would have a motive for kidnapping the young woman? Her own father, Barco, was of the amoral ilk to do such a thing, but what would he stand to gain from it? The company of his own daughter, I supposed, but if he was lonely for family affection he would surely not seek it through such forced means. Sending window-peeping ruffians to kidnap one's own daughter would hardly seem a likely route to winning back her heart after the offense of murdering the man she'd planned to marry.

So who else? I could think of only one likely option: Albert Flynn. Flynn hated Merry anyway and would have no qualms about subjecting her to a humiliating abduction. And he had something very practical to gain by holding her: he could demand from her father the return of the money stolen from the Repentance Creek bank, then stolen back again from David Flynn's blue carpetbag.

"Where is Charlie Crowder?" I asked the doctor.

"He is up and out . . . not hurt. He said he'd come back and check on your status in the morning."

"I won't be here."

"Beg your pardon?"

"I've got to leave . . . I have to join the hunt for the kidnappers."

"I suggest you rest. You've taken a battering of late, and your body needs the chance to heal."

"I've got to do this. Thank you for your help, Doctor. What do I owe you?"

"Your bill has already been paid by Mr. Walter Gage."

I might have guessed it. I quizzed the doctor, and the elderly man with the broom, about where the search was taking place.

They told me the posse, led by the sheriff, had begun at the site of the kidnapping and proceeded southwest from there. The old man, whose name was Frank Shaver, told me that the working theory of the posse was the one already stated by Dr. Greaves: that Merry had been kidnapped and hauled away for the purpose of a lewd assault.

I prayed they were wrong, for her sake.

13

With many warnings from the doctor that I was using bad judgment, I left the office and walked onto the street. It was very late, about one o'clock in the morning. I wondered where Merry was and what was happening to her, and also where those were who were pursuing her captors.

Wherever they were, I would join them. But there was one problem: I'd come to Anne Stover's house aboard Walter Gage's buggy. I had no horse, and just as importantly, no weapons beyond a pocketknife. I didn't even know how I'd been brought to the doctor's office — probably dumped into Gage's buggy again.

I wouldn't be much of a manhunter on foot, armed only with a short knife. I needed to find a horse and saddle, and arm myself.

Being still mostly unfamiliar with this town, it took me some time to get my bearings and figure out in which direction Anne's house lay. I set out walking, feeling at the moment none the worse for what I'd gone through. At this hour the town was sleeping, except for a couple of all-night saloons. I passed these by, figuring it highly unlikely that Merry's captors would show themselves in such a public place as a saloon, while their crime was still fresh. So I walked on past.

I reached Anne's house twenty minutes later, and was surprised to see the place still well-lighted. Gage's buggy was gone and I saw no one at all in the yard or on the road. I walked around to the front of the house, deliberately walking loudly so that I would surprise no one.

What a day! What a week! Arriving in Texas, looking for nothing but a meeting with Walter Gage, and I'd found myself embroiled in situations involving murder and robbery, and now a kidnapping and — God forbid — possibly worse than that. And despite my desire to pull myself away from this situation and move back into a more ordinary world, I was still officially deputized, and now manhunting again.

Had the entire world gone mad? Or just *my* world?

A shadow crossed the window. I wheeled

and looked at the house, and saw Anne looking back out. She was still dressed as she had been during the dinner, but had a frantic, frightened look on her face.

I couldn't tell for sure, but I did not believe she could see me. Reflexively I held still, obeying some primal impulse to remain invisible, but I didn't like the feeling that gave me. It made me feel much like that peeper outside Merry's window.

With her face close to the window, Anne squinted out into the darkness around me. At times she looked directly at me, but nothing indicated she saw me. Still, I kept completely still, even while considering just walking up to the door.

She turned away from the window and I was glad I had not done so. In her hand was a revolver.

But now I was left not knowing what to do. I could achieve nothing simply standing about in the dark. Suddenly I was sick of this inertia, this hiding out. I marched up to the house, onto the porch, and knocked on the door, firmly but not so strongly that it would sound alarming.

I sensed her presence on the other side of the door a few moments later, and saw the curtains on the little fan-shaped upper window on the door move. The lock rattled, the door shivered a little, then opened.

"Hello, Mr. Wells," she said. "I'm glad to see you up and around again."

"Call me Jed, please. And thank you. I'm glad to be up and around as well."

"I'd invite you in, but people around here like to talk, Jed. At this time of night, with no one else around . . ."

"Perhaps you can join me out here on the porch. Right here in the open, nothing to hide. I'd like to hear all that happened."

"There is still coffee hot on the stove . . ."

"I would love a cup, if you'll have one as well."

"I will. Please sit down . . . I'll be right back."

The coffee had grown strong and thick . . . but it brightened my mind and sharpened my senses. Ironically, being knocked senseless had provided me an opportunity to rest, that, combined with the coffee, left me quite alert for such a late hour.

I told her what I had heard, hoping she would inform me it was incorrect and that Merry was safely asleep in her house. But it was all true, and Merry was indeed kidnapped.

"I have a theory about who did it," I said.

"So do I," she replied. "Tell me your first."

"I believe that Albert Flynn is behind it,

194

and that a ransom demand will be made on Tate Barco — return the stolen money from the bank, and get back his daughter unharmed."

Her voice cracked a little; she had been crying before I got here. "I think you're right. That's my theory as well."

"I'm very worried about her," I admitted. "I think Albert Flynn has the potential to be a very evil man."

"More than potential, Jed. More than that. He already destroyed the happiness and life of his own son, and he has come to hate me and Merry because he associates us with Barco."

I could not dispute a word . . . her fears reflected my own.

"Where are they all?" I asked. "I understand the sheriff got involved."

"Yes. It was chance, or providence, depending on how you view such things. He was not a quarter mile away when the shots were fired . . . just riding through, heading for his home. He responded and even caught a glimpse of the kidnappers taking Merry away." Anne paused, bowed her head, said, "Oh, God!" and began to cry.

"Anne, what shots? I was never aware of any shots."

"It must have been after you were knocked

out, then. Other men, hidden beyond the hill, came up out of the dark while Charlie Crowder fought with the one you caught at the window. There were shots, fired at Mr. Crowder."

"Was he hit?"

"No, thank God. No. But Mr. Gage hit one of them. Whether by skill or luck, I couldn't guess."

"Wait — Walter shot one of them? Using what?"

"He had a pistol under his coat. I didn't know until he came out with it. He raised the window, aimed, and shot one of them. In the leg, I think."

"From that upper window, with a pistol . . . in the darkness?"

"Yes."

"That was a lucky shot, then. But luck is better than skill when you've got it. And Walter Gage has been lucky all his life."

"I love that man, Jed. He is to me the most perfect man I've ever met. His mind is sharp, his wit, his creativity . . . if only he had been younger. Or I had been older."

"Don't wish for age, Anne. Our time goes by fast enough as it is."

"It's not wishing for age . . . wishing for love, I suppose."

I had not expected such a personal level

of conversation. "Has there never been someone for you, Anne? Because as beautiful as you are, as appealing in so many ways, I would think there would have been many men eager to marry you."

I watched her eyes to see if I had delved into too intimate a subject area. At first I thought I had, but then her expression grew soft and open, and she smiled. "Thank you . . . there have been opportunities, had I wanted to pursue them. But I will never throw away my life by marrying the wrong man."

"You are as wise as you are beautiful," I said.

"If I were wise, surely I would have found a life that would not leave me so lonely."

"You need not be lonely," I replied. "You have a fine home in a good town, surrounded by people such as Walter Gage and Jim Clelland . . . and of course, Merry."

"I hope she is all right," Anne said, "I'm so worried about her."

"I need to join the search," I said. "But at the moment my horse and guns are back at the Clelland ranch."

"Do you really want to go out there, looking?"

"I must do it. I can't let a young woman be snatched away right from beneath my nose, and stand by and wait for her to be hurt."

"I have three horses, all in a livery stable one block from here. And a good saddle — a man's saddle, given to me by Jim Clelland, in fact . . . and I've got a good Winchester rifle, and a Colt pistol."

"Are you offering these for my use?"

"If you'll find Merry for me, you can *have* them."

"Just using them is all I ask. And if I can find her, I will. Unless the sheriff and Charlie and that posse have already done it. But tell me something: where does Albert Flynn live?"

"You'll not find Merry that way — Flynn is not fool enough to have her actually brought to his home."

"Any idea where, then?"

"No . . . no . . . not at all."

"Anne, I doubt I'll have much success finding her if I do nothing but ride out in the night and hope I stumble across her."

"Jed, I have no idea where to tell you to look."

"Where was Sheriff Strickland going to look?"

"I don't know . . . I think he was just following the Rockwell Road — that's the closest road to where the kidnappers were hidden, and I believe he thought that was the road they would take when they left."

"He may have found her by now, Anne. They may be on their way back right now."

"Oh, I hope . . . I hope!"

"So do I. May I take a look at that rifle now, Anne?"

"Where will you go? Where will you look?"

"I'll follow that road you mentioned . . . at the very least I might stumble across the posse and be able to join up with them. Otherwise, I'd be just riding random across the flatlands in the middle of the night, and the odds of finding Merry that way are about as slim as shooting into the sky with a blindfold on and hoping to hit a bird."

Out on the flatlands, a lone building stood along the side of a road — an island of light and activity on what should have been an empty plain. In my travels across the West I'd been mystified frequently by the question of why people chose to locate saloons at particular spots for no obvious reason. I'd ridden many a lonely road in many a locale, there to find some isolated watering hole standing where there was no community, no companion businesses, no apparent reason at all anyone should have stood and declared, "This is the place!"

Like many, this saloon was obviously an all-nighter. Here it was, long past midnight, and the place was going strong, spilling light and music and surrounded by hitched horses and parked wagons. Astonishing, really. This was cattle country, where men rose early and labored hard. How could anyone have the energy, or the time, to drink all night at such a random time? I rode near the saloon, which was named Carl's Beverages, and considered stopping in, just in case the kidnappers had been tempted to make a similar stop themselves. Unlikely, maybe . . . but this was no town saloon, where one would be readily spotted. This was the middle of nowhere.

I rode toward the place and watched a drunken cowboy stagger out and stumble off the porch, barely keeping his feet. He reeled and wobbled through a huge heap of horse manure and finally found his own horse, falling against it and keeping himself upright only by grabbing the saddlehorn.

"Are you going to make it, friend?" I asked him.

He turned his bleary eyes toward me. "If I can get into the saddle, I'll be all right. Horse knows the way home."

I boosted him up, and as I did so, spotted something I'd missed until now. Parked at the north side of the saloon was a familiar buggy, and its presence here told me an interesting story . . . the story of a valiant old publisher-turned-rancher who had left the scene of a kidnapping and all alone driven his buggy out onto the plains, ready to do what he could to help.

I watched the drunk ride off and hoped he'd be able to stay in his saddle. When he was out of sight, I turned to the door and entered the pool of light beyond it.

The place was busy for this time of the night. A lot of men, apparently, had developed a strong thirst this evening. My entrance drew no obvious attention; I was merely one more person among a score of others.

There he was! Walter Gage sat in the far corner of the saloon, sipping a beer. He noticed me while I stood looking at him, and rose. I walked toward him, winding between tables and dodging feet and table legs.

I passed a crowded table just as one of the men seated at it scooted back his chair and began to rise. My foot caught on the back leg of the chair and I stumbled a little, pivoting as I did so. As that happened, my eye fell on something lying on the tabletop, and I swear I almost froze in mid-stumble — it was one of those moments in which time and motion seem to stop.

But only seem to. In fact I kept tumbling, and almost took an embarrassing spill onto the floor, saving myself from it only by some fast footwork.

The man who'd scooted back the chair was a burly, bearded man, well over two-hundred pounds despite a lack of stature. He was a boulder on legs. He turned and grabbed my arms, helping stop me from falling, and his alcohol-reddened eyes looked right at me. "Mister, I'm mighty sorry," he said. "I didn't see you coming through there."

"No problem here," I said. "I'm not hurt."

He was looking at my wounded head. Though I had discovered that I could indeed hide the wound by carefully combing my hair, the night wind had moved my hair and the injury could be seen. "I think you are hurt, amigo," the man said.

"That's an old wound," I said. "I sure didn't get it from bumping into your chair. Don't worry about it." I gave him a friendly swat on the shoulder.

"You take care of yourself, friend," he said. "Let me buy you a beer."

I liked this man. "Thank you, sir, but you need not do it. I'd be obliged if you would give me one piece of information, though."

"Just ask."

"That rifle on the table . . . where did you get it?"

The rifle I was looking at was very familiar — I'd carried it enough years to know it when I saw it. And I'd seen it last when Tate Barco carried it away from the robbed stagecoach.

He looked worried. "I bought it, sir. Fair and square, honest purchase. I bought it from a feller."

"Sir, you come across to me as an honest man," I said. "I don't doubt you bought that rifle in the best of good faith. But I have to tell you that I recognize it. It's a rifle that I've had for many years, and in fact it was originally given to me by my father. It was stolen from me very recently."

"Oh, lordy, sir . . . I've bought a stolen rifle?"

"Unintentionally, I'm sure . . . but yes, you have."

"God . . . I should have known. Should have known!"

Another fellow at the same table, this one a runt with no hair on the top of his head, stood up and squinted at me through spectacles thick as the bottom of a wine bottle. "Rastus, you know who this man is?" he piped up in a high voice.

The first man shook his head and looked even more worried.

"This here is the fellow who was in the newspaper . . . the one who kilt Bailey Freeman and who took a shot at Tate Barco when that stagecoach was robbed."

Rastus obviously had read the paper, because his expression showed that he knew exactly what was being referred to. "Mister," he said. "I had no notion. None at all!"

"Don't worry about it . . . but I'd like to find a way to get my rifle back."

Rastus was a man in a diplomatic dilemma. He possessed a stolen item, but not one he'd stolen himself. He'd bought it as an honest purchase.

Someone cleared his throat nearby me. I glanced . . . Walter Gage was there. I suppose my stumbling incident had drawn his notice. He'd left his table and approached me.

"Hello, Walter," I said.

He nodded at me and looked at the rifle on the table. He'd seen that rifle before because he'd known me so long. He cleared his throat again.

"Yes, Walter?"

"Perhaps you'd let me talk to this gentleman on your behalf," he said.

I was puzzled, but this was Walter, so I nodded and stepped aside, going to the table Walter had left and sitting down there. I watched Walter talk intently to Rastus, then reach into his pocket and bring out a stack of bills. He and Rastus drew closer together, talking in whispers, now, and Walter handed Rastus some moncy. Rastus looked happy and gave Walter the rifle. Walter took it and came my way. He laid it on the table before me with a satisfied smile on his face.

"Your rifle, Mr. Wells."

14

"Walter, you bought that from him. What do I owe you?"

"Nothing, my friend. Not a cent. This is Walter you're talking to, remember? Walter who lends a hand to his friends whenever the opportunity arises! I would be insulted if you sought to recompense me for what was intended as a favor by a good friend. Now, excuse me a moment." He turned and caught up with Rastus, who was halfway to the door at this point. Rastus seemed startled and had that worried look again, but Walter brought out another bill, handed it to him, and that seemed to settle him down.

When it hit me why Walter had gone back to Rastus, I wondered if I'd been overly addled by being knocked unconscious earlier. I should have realized, as Walter obviously had, that Rastus having the rifle indicated a likely contact between him and

Tate Barco. He might be able to lead us, or at least point us, to Barco himself.

At the moment, though, I was much less concerned about finding Barco than finding Merry Gavin. Perhaps it was merely the passing of time, but my perspective was shifting; and now I saw Albert Flynn in more diabolical terms than Barco himself, though Baro's sins clearly were more abundant and serious. Barco was a murderer, more than once, and Flynn merely the sponsor of a kidnapping . . . assuming that was even the case. It could be that Flynn had no involvement in Merry's abduction at all. But I wasn't willing to bet on it.

Walter waved for me to come over. I picked up the rifle and went to him and Rastus, and Walter led us as a group out the door and into the yard among the hitched horses and parked wagons.

"Mr. Rastus here tells me he purchased the rifle not from Tate Barco, but from a man named Monty Carrey — a fellow I once had the misfortune to hire as a carpenter. Mr. Carrey is one of those small-level criminals of feeble mind who attach themselves to brighter ruffians such as Barco. Mr. Rastus tells me that Carrey informed him that Barco sold him the rifle, and Carrey hoped to make a profit from it. Mr. Rastus did not know that the rifle had been stolen by Barco, he says, and I believe him."

"So do I," I said, and a visible wave of relief passed over Rastus. My intuition that this was a man of good character grew stronger.

"Mr. Rastus," I said, "do you know where Barco might be found?"

"The same question I asked him," Walter cut in.

"I think I know where he *might* be," he said. "Don't know for sure . . . but Carrey told me he'd been out near the old saddlery when he bought the rifle. I think Barco hides out there some."

"What's the 'saddlery?' " I asked.

Walter jumped in before Rastus could reply. "The 'saddlery' is a local name for what was at one time a manufacturing facility, making saddles for a national market. Founded and funded by our old friend Albert Flynn, in fact."

"Flynn! And what became of this industry?"

"It failed, for reasons not entirely clear, but which I always believed resulted from malfeasance on Flynn's part."

"Dipping into the till for himself, was he?" Rastus asked.

"Precisely. Or so is my belief," Walter

answered. "In any case, his great experiment did not last long and the result is a huge, empty complex of buildings south of Repentance Creek the town, standing on the bank of Repentance Creek the waterway."

"A big, empty building . . . good possible place for a hideout."

"Correct, Jed. I should have thought of that before now."

"It would be ironic if Barco proved to be hiding in an old place once operated by Albert Flynn."

"Wouldn't it, though!"

"But we have to keep our thinking straight, Walter. We're not looking for Barco tonight . . . we're looking for Merry Gavin, and whoever has her."

"Yes . . . and the saddlery is just as likely a hideout for those ruffians as for Barco . . . perhaps more so if Flynn truly is behind the kidnapping."

"What if he isn't, Walter? What if there is some entirely different motive?"

"The motive for kidnapping is almost always money, is it not? And who associated with Merry has money? Certainly not Anne . . . and there really is no one else associated with her in this town, other than Anne, and her father Tate Barco."

"How widely known is it that Barco is her father?"

"I'm not certain . . . stories do tend to get around. But I don't think it is much known. Anne protects her closely, one of the things I admire about her. Merry is known by most simply as one of the two beautiful women who operate the local library."

"Walter, there is one other person who might be considered close to Merry . . . close enough that her protection might by that person be considered worthy of paying ransom."

"Who?"

"You, Walter. You are known as the chief benefactor of the library, and are seen as a man of great means. Not a false assessment, really. It might be believed that you would be willing to pay a sizeable ransom for the safe return of the library's own Merry."

"And so I would. But I have received no ransom demand."

"It could come yet."

"This talk makes me quite nervous, Jed."

"But you've already thought these thoughts yourself. You are too smart a man not to have done so."

"I admit it. I considered that terrible possibility almost from the outset. I hope it is not the case . . . no one wishes to be extorted for ransom . . . yet if it is me who is being targeted, in one way there is relief, because I will definitely pay what is required to buy her safety."

"I'm glad to hear you say it, but I hope it does not come to that."

"So do I. I hope we will simply find her free and well, and that none of this is what it appears."

"Let's go visit that big empty saddle factory."

"I'll drive my buggy . . . follow me. And keep aware . . . we could encounter trouble anywhere."

"You needn't tell me that. Trouble is most of what I've encountered ever since I set foot in Texas."

The building that once had housed the saddlery was bigger than I'd anticipated. It rambled on across the landscape, visible in the night mostly by merit of being darker than the landscape around it. Quite an enterprise Flynn had set up here! I wondered why it had failed. It was a logical industry for this part of the country, where saddles were ever in demand and hard to afford for many, and where the cattle business itself could provide a bountiful supply of leather to make the product.

"Well, Jed, here we are," Walter whispered. We'd come across a sweeping, shallow hill moments before, and now simply sat looking down at the big structure. I listened closely, seeking noises that would indicate human presence, and looking for movement in the darkness, flashes of match light, and so on. Nothing, though. The place looked and felt empty.

"Where is the entrance?" I asked.

"Facing east . . . we'll have to ride around the left side to see it. Huge double doors, like a barn. If they are open, we can look in."

"Let's go . . . but not in that buggy. Too loud. In fact, let's go down on foot, in case there are sentinels."

"You realize how dangerous this is, I hope."

"Yes . . . and when I do I have to make myself think of poor Merry, and how dangerous and frightening this must be for her."

"Indeed. A dear girl . . . sad she must endure this."

"Walter, if we find them, what do we do? There are only two of us, and we have no plan."

"If you are a praying man — and I believe you are, Jed — pray very hard. We'll figure this out as the facts of the situation become more clear."

We put my horse in a little stand of trees to my left and parked the wagon nearby as well, putting the trees between the wagon and the building so that it wouldn't be visible if a big burst of moonlight penetrated and lighted the landscape. Then we crept down, as silent as Indian scouts, and veered left to approach the east-facing side of the structure.

The moonlight did brighten some at that point, making us feel exposed but also giving us a good view of that side of the building. The big entrance was indeed standing open, but there was nothing to see inside but pure, cavern-like blackness. If anyone was hiding in there, they were doing so without benefit of lanterns.

"What do you think, Jed?"

"I think that this would make a good place to hide, as you said . . . but I see no evidence to make me think anyone is here but us."

"I agree," he said, sounding disappointed. "I had hoped that by some miracle we would encounter them, and by some other miracle find a way to rescue Merry."

"That's a lot of miracles to hope for in one night," I commented.

"Yes . . . an over-abundance of faith on

213

my part, I suppose."

"Should we go in, in case they are hiding in there?"

Walter drew nearer the door and peered inside. I did the same. Nothing! Just a great, black hole.

"Walter, are we looking into one vast empty chamber, or are there walls and rooms back in there, breaking up the space?"

"My memory is that the front half of the building is one space, with a wall across the interior about halfway back, dividing the place. Beyond that wall, I think, are rooms for storage, as well as office spaces and so on."

"So someone could be on the far side of that wall, and we would not see them."

"Possibly . . . but we have no positive evidence that this is the case."

We entered the building, just a few yards, listening more than looking because ears were better than eyes in such darkness. Walter was only a few feet away and I could hardly tell he was there. At last he spoke, in a whisper.

"Let's leave here, Jed, and get back to our places. If a ransom demand does come to me, I should be home to receive it, not out roaming the countryside."

This made sense, and I agreed: Walter, at least, should be accessible, and therefore should return home. My situation was different. No ransom demand would come to me, so I could do more good out "roaming the countryside" than by lodging in my room at Clelland's ranch.

But for the moment I would stick with Walter, riding back with him to his home, just in case we happened to run across the sheriff and his posse, or even the kidnappers themselves. We left the big building and headed back up the low hill to where my horse and Walter's buggy awaited. I took one final glance back at the building as I mounted up — and noticed something momentary but significant.

A flash of light, dim, visible as if through a knothole in the wall, coming from somewhere deep inside. Someone had struck a light, but not for long. In fact, I wasn't even sure I'd seen it.

"Walter, I think I saw a light in the building," I said.

"Really? I don't see anything."

"It was just a flash of light, like someone striking a match or carrying a lamp past a hole in the wall."

"More likely, Jed, your eyes played tricks on you. Or maybe it was a firefly."

"Maybe so." Truly I couldn't be certain.

"Let's roll. Perhaps we'll find good news along the way, eh?"

"Perhaps."

We rode off, me wondering if I was doing the right thing. I couldn't swear that light I'd seen wasn't a trick of my eyes or a misidentification of something natural, but I didn't think it was. I was a sharpshooter, accustomed to viewing things at a long distance and trained in how to interpret visual information.

I was nearly certain I'd seen a light in that big building. After I parted from Walter, maybe I'd return and take a closer look. If Merry was in there, I'd do what I had to do to get her out.

The ride to Walter's ranch home took more than an hour. I was surprised that it did not tire me more, and could attribute my stamina only to the rest I'd received before waking up in Dr. Greaves' care.

Walter invited me to make a bed of his sofa and rest out the remainder of the night, but I still felt drawn to the search for Merry. I could not consider sleeping when I did not know where she was or what she was suffering at the hands of her still-unknown captors. And I could not get that perhaps-imagined glimmering of light back at the saddlery out of my mind.

"I'll go, and hope I can stumble upon the posse," I told Walter. "I feel obliged to continue."

"Then do so. I would join you if not for the possibility that doing so would leave me unavailable should the kidnappers contact me."

I took my leave of my old friend, and began the long ride back in the direction from which we'd come.

I took my time on the long ride back to the saddlery building, conscious of my solitary situation and unsure just what I would do when I reached the place, anyway. Would I simply walk in, rifle at ready, and face off with whoever was there, if there was anyone there at all?

More likely, I'd set up watch of the place and wait to see someone emerge.

My horse hidden by the same grove as before, I found a place beneath one of the scrubby trees and settled onto the ground. The contours of the earth at that spot were such as to accommodate a human form as if made to do so, and I grew quite comfortable there. Before long my eyes began to droop and my breathing to slow. Weariness was setting in and sleep crept up on me. I fought it, but before long I was lying still and quiet, eyes closed, slumbering peacefully despite the setting and circumstances.

I awakened and found the world changed. The first glimmerings of daylight were spreading across the sky and landscape. I sat up, muddleheaded and bleary-eyed, and tried to make sense of my situation. Where was I and how had I gotten here?

It all came back quickly when I looked down and saw the sprawling old saddle manufacturing building below me on the flats. In daylight it didn't seem quite as vast as it had looked in the darkness, but it was indeed a big structure. There was much not to admire about Albert Flynn, but I couldn't fault his cleverness and enterprise for seeking to create an industry in this area where the cattle trade so dominated. Too bad it hadn't worked out.

I heard motion in the grove of trees behind me. Thinking my horse had worked its way into the grove as far as its tether would allow, I turned. . . . And my heart jumped to full speed in half a second.

I was staring into the muzzle hole of a rifle, no more than a foot from my head. I backed away a couple of steps and looked at the face of the man holding the rifle. My heart hammered even faster.

"Hello, 'hero,' " said Tate Barco. "That's what the paper called you, you know. The big 'hero' who dared take a shot at wicked Tate Barco! Looks like the hero has really stepped into it this morning, don't it now!"

15

"What's your name, hero? Wells, ain't it? Then tell me, Mr. Wells, why the hell are you out here this morning? You been looking for me? You still playing 'manhunter'?"

Somehow I found my voice. "No, sir, I've not been hunting for you. I'm hunting for someone else . . . your daughter, Merry. She's been kidnapped."

Clearly he'd not expected to hear something like that. He blinked like a man with sweat stinging his eyes, stammered a little, and said, "What did you say?"

"I said, Merry Gavin has been kidnapped. She was taken from her own residence by a group of men, earlier this very night. Several people are trying to find her, and I thought this might be a likely place someone might hide her. I saw a light inside the building down there earlier. I guess it was *your* light, though, not kidnappers."

"No, not me. I've hid there before, but

not now. I've got me a different place. God! Why would anyone take Merry?"

"We don't really know for sure. Some suspect she was taken for misuse, God forbid. Me, I think there'll be a demand for ransom."

"Made upon who?"

"Maybe upon you."

He pondered that, his rifle lowering. I'd suddenly become too interesting to shoot.

"Did you have something to do with this, Wells? Are you trying to get your hands on my money?"

"No, sir. I tried to stop it from happening, and got myself knocked senseless for it."

"How do you know about Merry? Ain't a lot of folks know I've got a daughter."

"More know than you might realize." I hesitated at this point. Though I had a plausible theory about what was behind the kidnapping, theory was all it was, not fact. I didn't want to blame Flynn without knowing he was really responsible. Barco was a violent man who might react against Flynn without waiting for the facts to clarify. Flynn resolved my dilemma with his next words. "Albert Flynn knows about her," he said. "Albert Flynn knows!"

"Yes," I said. "He does. He spoke to me of it."

"I would guess you as a friend of Flynn's . . . you seem the kind."

That offended me more than he could know. "I'm no friend of Flynn's," I said. "I have no regard for him or how he treated his own flesh and blood. He may prove as evil a man as you are, in his own way."

"Oh, I'm a real bad man, no doubt of that!" He chuckled. "But what has Flynn done to make you think the same of him?"

Here was where I had to be careful not to make an open accusation I couldn't prove. "For one thing, I despise how he treated his son . . . crying and tearful as they buried him, but treating him scornfully in life, as I'm told it."

"Hell, that damned boy was as bad as his father, and I'm glad he's dead. One less Flynn in this world."

"I would think you would like David Flynn better than that. I'm given to understand that he orchestrated a bank robbery for you to carry out. He got revenge against his miserable father — and you got money."

"Quite a trick, eh? Father makes boy mad, boy gets vengeance by cleaning out his father's bank! Left old man Flynn in a pickle, for the fool had promised several of his biggest depositors that he would personally guarantee their accounts against robbery. So he had to make up from his own pocket a part of what was took!"

"Yes . . . but the situation didn't hold . . . David Flynn was persuaded to attempt to make peace with his father and decided to return the money to him, or as much of it as he could get his hands on."

Barco's eyes narrowed. "Aye, yes . . . with the help of my own flesh and blood, he tried to do that very thing."

"Merry helped him . . . Merry, I think, was the very one who stole back the bank money from you, and gave it to David to return."

"Yes . . . yes . . . but neither that Judas child of mine nor that fool son of Devilish Flynn counted on me and Hiram stealing it back!"

"And in the process, murdering three people, robbing several others, and injuring me."

"How is it murder, when you're only trying to defend yourself?"

"How do you see what you did as defending yourself — to shoot a stagecoach guard and driver who are doing nothing but their jobs?"

"Because that guard fired the first shot at me, that's why! I was doing nothing but sitting by a roadside, watching the stage pass,

223

and he up and shot at me!"

"So you blasted him off his seat and under the wheels of the stagecoach."

"He fell where he fell . . . that wasn't anything I could control."

"What about David Flynn? He was not threatening you when you killed him."

"No . . . but it wasn't him I shot at . . . it was at you, Mr. Hero Wells, you who aimed a rifle at me out the stagecoach window!"

"So you see that as self-defense as well?"

"I see the death of young Flynn as a fortunate accident that occurred during an act of self-defense."

"A fortunate accident?"

"The young bastard betrayed me . . . trying to take away from me the fruits of my work."

"So bank robbery is work?"

"I challenge you to try it sometime, then try to tell me that it isn't!"

"I have no intention to take up such a dishonest trade, sir."

"Well, there's another star in your crown, hero!"

"Barco, let's stop babbling and bickering at each other and consider the one interest we have in common: we want to get your daughter back safe and sound. I'm willing to help you do that . . . but if I'm right about what is behind this, you'll have to be willing to give up the money you stole."

"I know what you're thinking," he said. "You're thinking that Flynn has had my daughter taken so that he can demand his money back from me in return for her safety."

"That *is* what I'm thinking . . . but I don't know it is true."

"Well, it makes sense to me," he said. "This is just the sort of wickedness that old miser would do! If my daughter is taken, then he's the one who did it."

"If so, he'll have to make a ransom demand on you . . . but he doesn't know where to find you . . . you're not a man who can let himself be seen much in public. How will he get the ransom demand to you?"

"He'll figure out a way . . . but he won't have to. I'm going to go to him and spare him the trouble of trying to find me."

"You're going to Flynn?"

"Yes . . . and you'll go with me. I need a hostage to keep me safe, and you'll do fine."

I had my doubts. Flynn, in the end, had little reason to care what happened to me . . . I would probably not afford Barco much protection.

"Barco, do you think that Merry might be down there in that big building? She's got to be hidden somewhere, and I doubt Flynn would keep her at his own dwelling. . . . There's too much implication of guilt in doing that."

"Listen, Wells, if you think I'm going to go riding down there with you and waltz into that building down there to perform some big rescue, it ain't going to happen. I don't even know that what you're telling me is true . . . Merry might be safe in her own home for all I know."

"I swear to you, Barco, she was taken. I witnessed it all, even fought with some of the abductors. I can understand why you wouldn't trust me, but I vow it's the truth. And the best thing you could do is exactly what you're thinking — go talk face to face with Albert Flynn, and see if you can determine whether he is the guilty party. If he is — and I suspect he is just like you do — then we can find out what it will take to get her out safely again."

"I may be a fool to trust you, Wells, but I'm going to do it. I'll take you at your word that Merry is kidnapped, and I'll take the risk of going to Flynn himself. But hear me: if I find that you've lied to me, I'll kill you. I'll kill you before Flynn's eyes, and kill him as well."

"Barco, listen: I don't know that Flynn is

226

guilty, and if he isn't, he may not even be aware that Merry was taken. But she was, she was. Someone took her for whatever reason. Flynn is the most obvious suspect, but she could have been taken for other, fouler, reasons, by anyone. She's a pretty young woman, and there are men out there, as you know, who have no sense of decency or respect."

His face gave a little spasm, as if in pain. "I won't hear of such a thing . . . not regarding *my* little girl, no sir!"

"Are you and Merry close?" I asked, though I already knew the answer to that at least from Merry's point of view.

"Merry ain't ever been much proud of her papa," he said. "She'd rather I'd been a preacher or a schoolmaster or a store owner than what I am."

"Do you blame her for that, Barco? Especially now that you've killed the man she loved?"

"Like I said . . . just an accident."

"One you and your partner celebrated after it was done."

"I don't grieve that dead boy. I hated him, like I hated his father. Now, enough talk. Let's ride. We're going to visit Albert Flynn, and see how much truth there is in what you've said to me."

16

Barco seemed substantially unconcerned as we rode. The night began to wane, the first glimmerings of sun coming over the horizon. We were no longer hidden in darkness. Barco was taking quite a risk by riding on an open road in rising daylight, and toward a town, where potential witnesses would be abundant.

Clearly he took what I told him seriously. Otherwise he'd not be taking such a risk.

I felt exposed. Barco had disarmed me back on the hillside, so I was riding along unprotected, in the company of a wanted criminal.

"What's your plan?" I asked him. "Can you just ride up to Flynn's door without somebody blasting you out of the saddle along the way? We're visible out here, you know."

"Hell, don't you know yet that half the folks in these parts think I'm the finest man since Robin Hood? You know about him, don't you . . . hard on the rich and mean, good to the common folks. That's me. I'm good to those who deserve it. You know that money I got from the big rich depositors at the Repentance Creek bank? You think I've kept it all for myself? No sir . . . I gave three hundred dollars to a widow over north of town who was about to lose her house because she couldn't pay her mortgage . . . a mortgage held by Albert Flynn, by the way. So I use what money I gain not only to help myself, but others, too. The ones I help are good people. Common folks, not the rich uppity ones like them who call Flynn their friend."

"But some common folks — say, stage-coach drivers and guards — tend to not fare quite so well with you, do they?"

He snarled and looked sour, but did not attempt a reply to what was obviously a very strong point.

We rode into town, encountering no one until we rounded a corner and headed toward a large near-mansion that could only be Flynn's home. A young boy with a carved wooden pistol strapped to his hip in an obviously homemade holster looked up at Barco. "Hello, Mr. Barco!" he said in a tone of admiration. "How are you, sir?"

"Hello, boy," Barco said. "I'm fine. Hope you are, too. Tell me something — any sign of life around the banker's house there?"

"Old Man Flynn's house, you mean? Yes, sir. I saw the housemaid going out to the henhouse for eggs as the sun was coming up. And there's been a light burning up in the top floor since a long time before daylight . . . and one way up in the attic, too."

"You know anything about the layout of that house, son?" I asked.

"Well, I been in it once with my dog — he's a rat-catching dog, and Old Man Flynn had a rat that had got in there, so he told me he'd give me a dollar if my dog could catch it."

"Did he?"

"Hell yes, he caught that rat after we run it all over the house . . . but then old Flynn just told me to get my hind end out of his home, and didn't give me a *cent* to pay for the ratting! All he gave me was a piece of cold chicken left over from his supper the night before. It didn't even taste good. I hate that cheap old bastard!"

"Strong words from such young lips," I said. "What's in the attic?"

"Nothing much . . . it's just like most attics. Old rubbish, some furniture he don't use downstairs, you know."

"Odd that a light would be burning up there so early in the morning, then," I said. "Maybe we should take a look for ourselves up in that attic."

"What? You think he'd have her up there?" Barco asked. "He'd not keep her on his own place! You said so yourself."

"I did . . . but what if I'm wrong? A light in the attic merits a look, just in case."

"How do you plan to get up there?"

"By making like my friend Charlie Crowder. The man can climb like an organ grinder's monkey. You saw him do it yourself, Barco, while that stage was running loose without a driver. If he can do it, so can I."

My eye was on a heavy trellis that ran up the side of the big house almost to the base of a round attic window, hinged on one side, latched on the other. The trellis crossed no lower windows and appeared likely to provide access to the upper levels of the house without excessive risk of being seen.

"You or me?" I asked Barco.

"I ain't going up that thing," he said. "I ain't no monkey, and I sure as hell don't want to be caught inside Flynn's house."

"So it's me, then." I dismounted and trotted across the yard, keeping hidden from the house by means of a hedge and line of small trees that served as ornamentation in the yard. If Flynn was in there, I didn't want him seeing me before I was ready . . . and I certainly didn't want him seeing me with Barco.

I reached the trellis and tried my weight on the bottom horizontal piece. It creaked a little but held. I went up two or three levels with no bad result. The trellis pulled back slightly as I climbed, but held in place. Up I clambered . . . feeling a little more scared the more I thought about what I was doing and my vulnerability on many levels should I be caught.

Finally I reached the top of the trellis. Before me was the round window. I peered through the wavy glass, which was dirty, dark, and partially obscured on the inside by a white cotton curtain. No hope of seeing anything clearly in there.

The latch, naturally, opened from the inside, but with my pocketknife blade I was able to loose it from outside. I pulled the window open and climbed through it, into the shadowed attic.

I wondered just what I was doing, and if I'd lost my mind. Did I really believe I'd find Merry as easily as this, conveniently tucked away in Albert Flynn's attic?

It was blind hopefulness, I suppose. . . . Or maybe a wish to separate myself from Barco any way I could. I could only imagine what might happen if Flynn looked out his window and saw his most hated nemesis there in his own yard. On the other hand, at this point he might be glad to have access to him, if there was in fact a ransom demand waiting to be delivered.

I'd expected the attic to be open across the entire top of the house, but in fact it was partitioned into rooms. The one I was in was dirty and rather small, stacked with crates and typical household items of the sort too good to throw out but not good enough to use. And there was a bed up here, just a small bunk, neatly made, and a few items of furniture. A place for Flynn to steal an afternoon nap on cool afternoons? A lodging place for unwanted guests? I couldn't imagine sending a *wanted* guest to such a dismal lodging as this.

Lightly as I could, I took a step. Instantly and loudly the floor creaked and snapped so loudly I was sure it would be heard all through the house. It made me wince. Another step, another creak, but this time not so loud.

Well, here I was, in the house . . . but so what? I had to admit to myself that what had driven me up that trellis was the long-shot hope that the attic light the boy had seen really had meant I would find Merry up here, ready for an easy rescue. Absurdly optimistic, obviously.

Should I go back down the trellis and take my chances with Barco? Or might it be better to go ahead and be found up here, and talk directly to Flynn without Barco's immediate presence?

The latter option seemed more reasonable. Even though I was an intruder in this house, and Flynn or one of his servants could have me arrested or even gun me down as a burglar, I still felt less at risk on my own than in the company of Barco, whom Flynn already despised so deeply.

I walked across the creaking floor to the door that led out of the room. Beyond it I found a shadowed hallway, unpainted and rough, and at the end of that another door that opened to a narrow stairway angling down to the third floor of this tall house.

Down there somewhere would be Albert Flynn, unless he was one of those kinds who went to his workplace at absurdly early hours.

The scent of cooking bacon reached my nose. Someone down there was making breakfast. I was quite hungry and the scent was distracting.

At the base of the stairs I paused at the final door, and simply listened. No footfalls on the other side, no muffled voices. I opened the door an inch and peered out into a carpeted hallway. At its side was a banister and beyond that a big, empty expanse of house interior. I opened the door further and went out. I was on the highest finished level of the house, on the landing, looking down through the great open area that extended from the entrance below all the way to the ceiling, above which was the attic I'd just left. Flynn had a magnificent house indeed, though one that surely grew quite cold in the winter, for it would take much to heat this big, open space.

I stood by the banister, hoping to see but not be seen. But there was no immediate stirring of human life below. A big house-dog, lazy and old, wandered across the entranceway floor below, paused, sniffed the air, probably catching the distant scent of an unfamiliar intruder — me.

But the beast did not look up, bark, or otherwise give me away. I waited and watched some more, then saw a woman cross the floor below — a woman in a domestic's uniform, carrying a duster in her left hand and a rubbish bucket in her right.

She nudged the dog to the side with one foot as she passed, and was clearly oblivious to the presence of a watching stranger in the house.

Five minutes went by, with no other developments than the woman crossing the same space again in the opposite direction, an intensification of the aroma of the cooking bacon, and a manservant strolling below me on the second level landing. He too did not detect me.

But clearly I was going to have to make my presence known to someone if I hoped to talk to Flynn independently of Barco. This seemed crucial to me; I was nearly sure that Flynn would not meet Barco without one or the other of them resorting to violence.

The issue was how to reveal my presence without generating panic. I decided that the best approach would be to try to sneak down to the entrance area below, out the front door onto the porch, and there to knock and seek entrance in the usual fashion. Whether I could do this without being caught by one of the servants was the unanswered question.

I turned to head for the stairs, and the whole issue became moot. A bedroom door nearby opened and a young servant girl

stepped out, carrying old bed linens des-
tined for the laundry room. She did not
scream when she saw me — though I had
to restrain a yell myself — but she did let
out a loud gasp, stagger back, and drop her
bundle of linens. She froze at that point, her
freckled face a mask of fear as she gaped at
this intruder into her home and workplace.

"Miss," I said. "Don't be afraid. I'm here
to see Mr. Flynn, and apologize for having
startled you."

"How . . . how did you get up here?" she
asked, struggling to keep her voice from
squeaking in her nervousness.

"Miss, I came down from above . . . I
climbed the trellis up to the attic window.
It's hard to explain why I did that, but I
was looking for someone. I had reason to
believe that a young woman named Merry
Gavin might be a . . . guest in this house,
and I thought I might find her there in that
room."

"Merry Gavin. . . . Oh, God, who are you?
Why are you looking for her? You are not
the outlaw Tate Barco, are you?"

"No, Miss. My name is Wells. Jed Wells."

She was an auburn-haired girl with the
fair complexion of a red-haired person, and
her pale, freckle-spotted face blanched even
more when she heard my name. She stepped

237

back, now completely inside the room she'd exited when she first encountered me. I stepped forward, to the door, but did not enter the room with her, conscious of appearances and propriety, and not wishing to scare her further.

"You are Jed Wells?" she said in a breathless whisper. "Are you the Jed Wells who killed my uncle Bailey?"

Good Lord, I'd just encountered one of the Freeman clan!

"I must admit to you that I am, Miss, but I did not do it because I wanted to. I was trying to protect the life of the sheriff, and my own life. Your uncle seemed ready to kill us both."

Her expression underwent a transformation as I spoke. The fear vanished from her brown eyes and she smiled. "Sir, my name is Sarah Franks, and I must tell you that I am honored to meet you. I am honored to meet any man who rid the world of such a monster as the man who beat my poor aunt so badly, so many times."

Now, here was a twist I'd not expected!

"Is Bailey Freeman your uncle by blood, or by marriage?"

"By marriage, sir. He married my mother's sister . . . and God knows no dog should have to endure being treated the way he treated her all the years of their marriage. I am glad for her sake that he is gone . . . glad that you killed him, sir."

I could think of nothing to say to that . . . but it came to mind that I might be able to gain information from this girl, admiring of me as she was.

"Miss, I'm sorry I was forced to kill your uncle . . . but I'm glad that your aunt is better off for it. That provides much further sense of justification for what I had to do. Now, do you mind if I privately ask you a few questions . . . not about your aunt, but about this place you work, and Mr. Flynn?"

"Sir, would you think it wrong of me if I asked you to speak to me inside this room, with the door closed? I can't risk Mr. Flynn seeing me talk to you, or talking about him at all. He can be a very hard and stern man, and he countenances no gossip about him among his servants."

"But my guess is that the gossip takes place anyway."

"Like my mother says, sir, that's just simple human nature."

"Is your mother also a servant here?"

"She is a cook, sir. She is finishing Mr. Flynn's breakfast even now."

"I smell the bacon. I'll wager she is a very fine cook, and a very fine mother for you."

"Oh, yes, sir." She smiled at me quite warmly. "And she is as grateful to you as I am for ridding us of Uncle Bailey. She used to cry at night, knowing her sister was being hurt by him."

How odd it was to be thanked by someone for killing a relative! It gave me a soul-soiled feeling, despite the fact Bailey Freeman had clearly been a bad man.

"Mr. Wells, if I can help you find what you've come looking for, I'll do it."

"Thank you, Miss . . ."

"I'm Agatha."

"Miss Agatha." Now I hesitated. Could I truly be honest with this girl? What I had to say had serious ramifications, and should it get back to Flynn, I didn't know what would happen. Especially if my suspicions and Barco's were misplaced.

What the devil! I had no choice but to ask . . . and who better than a house servant to know what was going on in a particular household?

"Miss, I must ask you to swear to secrecy about what I ask you. It is a question, not a statement of fact, and I would not have a hurtful falsehood spread because of something I said."

"Mr. Wells, you have my solemn word."

She said it so seriously, so deeply, that I

almost wanted to laugh. Instead I nodded and looked back at her just as solemnly.

"Very well. Agatha, a young woman of this town has been kidnapped. I am concerned for her safety and trying to find her and free her. You understand what I mean by kidnapped?"

"Yes, sir. She's been taken away by somebody she didn't want to go with."

"That's correct. And we don't yet know who did it. But there is a theory, an idea, that it might be someone who wants to exchange her for money. And because the kidnapped young woman is the daughter of a noted outlaw, some of us think that perhaps the person who kidnapped her was once robbed by that outlaw, and wants to get the stolen money back again in exchange for freeing the girl."

"Sir," Agatha said, "are you maybe talking about the pretty lady at the library, the younger one?"

"You know about this?"

"I know that her name is Merry Gavin, and I wish I was half as pretty as she is."

"Agatha, you are a lovely young woman, and I'm sure are envied by many other girls yourself."

She shook her head and looked very sad.

"You are right about Merry Gavin being

the kidnapped young woman."

"And her father is Tate Barco. Not everybody knows that, but it's true."

"Yes . . . it is true."

"So you think somebody that Tate Barco robbed has kidnapped her?"

"It's a possibility."

"I think it's the truth, Mr. Wells. And I think I know who did it."

"Are we in that man's house right now?"

Her eyes welled up. "I'm afraid to speak so . . . I'll get in such trouble if I get caught!"

"I'll not betray you, Agatha. You have *my* solemn word."

"Yes . . . Mr. Flynn did it, sir. I'm sure of it. I heard him talking to some men about two days ago. They were planning it. Tate Barco robbed Mr. Flynn's bank, you know. Mr. Flynn wants to get even with him."

"Yes. Are you sure you heard them specifically talking about a kidnapping? Did they call the name of Merry Gavin?"

"No . . . but they talked about the 'pretty book gal.' That's what the men talking to Mr. Flynn called her. Mr. Flynn called her something else, though . . . a name I shouldn't say. But it's a word in the Bible."

"Agatha, you have just provided me the most important information I could have received from anyone today. Now tell me: is

Mr. Flynn in the house right now?"

"Yes, sir. We're just past his breakfast time. He'll go to his bank about 8:30."

"Do you think there is a way I could talk to him without him having me arrested for being in his house?"

"You could go out again, and come to the door. I'll let you in if you knock, and you can ask to see him."

A smart young woman. And right-thinking: the direct approach would be best. "I'll do that, Agatha. I'll go back down the trellis and meet you at the front door."

She nodded and put out her hand for me to shake, as if we'd just concluded an important transaction. I grinned at her and shook her small hand firmly.

She played guard for me as I made my way secretly back to the staircase leading into the attic. I quickly got back to the window and headed back down the trellis after looking around to make sure no one from the house was in the yard. I could not see Barco; he'd hidden, or maybe even left.

17

The trellis seemed less stable as I went down. I suppose trellises wear out under such use, which is hardly what they are made for. But it held and I made it to the ground. A quick look around — no Barco. Forgetting him for the moment, I went to the front door, straightened my clothing, and knocked.

Agatha had the door open in a moment. "Good morning, Miss!" I said, speaking loudly and as if I had not already met her, for I knew others would probably hear me. I told her I had come on business with Mr. Flynn and requested entrance to see him.

Agatha was an efficient lass, and within five minutes I was walking through the door to Flynn's personal dining room, where he sat at the table sipping coffe with the remnants of his breakfast still before him.

"Hello, Wells," he said with thinly veiled contempt. "What the hell brings you out this morning? Coffee, by the way?"

"I'll take a cup, thank you."

He called for a servant, and a maid who strongly resembled Agatha came through a swinging doorway. He gruffly ordered her to bring me coffee, and she politely nodded to him, and to me, and set off to do it. She was back in less than a minute.

The coffee was rich and strong, the kind I liked best. I drank it black, unlike Flynn, whose cup held so much milk mixed with the coffee that the beverage was more nut-colored than black.

"Speak up, Wells!" he demanded, drumming his fingers on the tabletop. "Why are you here?"

"I'm here to tell you something you may already know, and something you certainly do not know."

"Riddles! Talk straight to me, man!"

I deliberately took a slow, long sip of coffee, letting him stew a few extra moments. "Here's what you may know already: there has been a kidnapping. Merry Gavin was taken in the night from her own home. It is not known by whom, but I and others saw at least some of them and even fought with them. And a sheriff's posse set out on their track right after the abduction."

"I'll be damned!"

I couldn't resist saying "I think that's a likely possibility, from what I've observed of you."

"Now, how would you expect that I would know already about this kidnapping?"

"Because I think you may have sponsored it."

"Now, *there's* a strong accusation! Accusing me of a crime, you are! I'll see you in court for slander."

"I doubt you'd want this affair looked into as deeply as a court case would cause it to be," I replied. "I believe you kidnapped Merry Gavin so you could demand from her father the money he robbed from your bank . . . money he ultimately robbed out of your own pocket because of the recompense you made to your depositors. I salute you for that, by the way."

"Oh, how touched I am! Saluted by the very man who just labeled me an abductor of young women!"

"Just one young woman . . . one young woman you despise and who has a strong connection to the man you despise worst of all."

"So you figure I'm trying to get my money back any way I can. Just a hypothetical question: if that were true, could you blame me for it?"

"I could blame you for it, yes. It's a vile thing to carry off a young woman in such a manner. God only knows what she's being put through."

"I'm quite certain that those who have her know that the consequences will be severe should they misuse her in any fashion."

"I'd say you *are* quite certain of that."

"Judge me as you will, say what you will, even have that newspaper that worships you so make accusations, if you want. I admit nothing. But I will say this: I can give you assurance that, should Tate Barco return that which he stole, he can be sure his daughter will not be harmed. And if he does not, that she will be harmed indeed."

"As good as a confession, Flynn. Do you think me a fool? You deny involvement, then make statements that imply not only involvement, but control of the situation! We both know you did it."

"You told me there was something you had to say that I do not know about. What is it?"

"Simply that I have established contact with Barco. I can get your demand to him. He already believes you the culprit, by the way. And I agree with him."

"I'm shattered, deeply." He grinned mockingly and took another slurp of his weakened coffee, before going on: "If you are in contact with that bastard, then pass along to him what I told you. And this does not imply that I am the instigator of this abduction, Wells. I simply am claiming a certain amount of influence, something a man in my position is accustomed to."

"I think it will take more than being a noted citizen to influence a band of kidnappers," I suggested, not believing for a moment he was anything but completely guilty of the crime, from planning to whatever the finish would be.

"The best you can do, sir, is simply deliver the message to the bastard who needs to hear it," he told me. "I don't know what has aligned you with that devil, but you provide me a convenience by serving as my conduit of information to him."

"I will see he hears what you demand," I said.

"And Wells . . . stay away from the newspaperman, will you? If you complicate this matter, it can only go worse for the girl."

"Not that you are controlling this situation, correct?"

"Correct."

I could not believe the man could not realize how transparent he was. No court in the land would leave him unconvicted if it heard all he'd just said to me.

I rose, finishing off my coffee and thanking him for it. "How would you want the money delivered?" I asked.

"Here," he said. "To this house, to this hand." He held up his right hand, wiggling the fingers.

"We shall see what Barco replics, shall we not?" I told him, smiling coldly.

"I have a feeling that those holding his daughter are wicked and sensual men . . . if he loves his girl, he'd best be a cooperative chap."

"I'll tell him. But I think he is already aware that his daughter has fallen victim to a very wicked man."

He understood what and whom I meant, and with that thought lingering behind, I left the room and headed for the door.

Barco was safely hidden behind a shed, with the horses. He said nothing, letting his eyes ask the question.

"He gave me the ransom demand, and it is what we anticipated," I said. "He wants back what was taken."

"I already told you that some of it is gone."

"I think that if the most part of it is returned he will be satisfied. If not, I will seek to make up the difference myself, and perhaps with the help of others who care what happens to Merry."

He nodded.

"You should know that Flynn denies any involvement in the kidnapping," I said. "I think he's lying, but he claims he had nothing to do with it, but still has 'influence' over what will happen in its resolution."

"He's a lying son of a bitch . . . always has been."

"I tend to think you're right."

"So he wants his money, does he?"

"Yes . . . delivered to his hand at his house."

"If he wants me to walk in there, it ain't going to happen."

"I think he expects me to deliver it."

One of his brows went almost straight up, the other going down, giving him an odd and very skeptical look. "You want me to just hand you that money and turn you loose with it?"

"Mr. Barco, I'm not going to take that money. I want to see Merry Gavin freed and safe. I think we should do this as Flynn directs and not tamper with the plan. He's a dangerous man, and I don't want to put a spark to his fuse, if you know what I mean."

"I know. What the hell — you don't seem the stealing kind. I'll trust you."

"But where is the money? Do you carry it on you, in your saddlebags, maybe?"

"I did for a brief while, until I found a good hiding place for it. You won't guess where."

I took a wild shot. "At the saddlery."

"Jehosaphat, boy, you guessed it right off! It's hid there . . . not easy to find, and nobody knows where to look but me."

"Let's go get it now. The sooner we get this done, the sooner Merry will be safe."

"She ain't going to *be* safe just because of some money. Not with Flynn."

"What do you mean?"

"It ain't just about money for Flynn. Nor for me, truth be told. It's about pride, too. And that's why he'll want more than the money back. He'll want me, too. Locked up, and if possible, waiting for the hangman."

Those words reminded me of something I was tending to forget, now that I was dealing with Barco one on one, man to man. That was that this man, who actually was now harder to hate than before, was a violent murderer. He deserved the hangman. And that, ultimately, was the basis upon which Barco would have to be dealt with: as a murderer of innocent men, *not* as a man who had merely injured the pride of an arrogant banker.

But at the moment, what mattered was Merry Gavin. Whatever it took to get her safe again had to be done.

"Well, here's the question, Barco: are you going to do it or not? Are you going to turn over that money, and if you have to, yourself, to get your daughter safe again?"

He gave me a wry look. "Let's go to the saddlery and see what kind of money we can turn up."

"We're likely to turn up a lot of trouble as well."

"So we are."

From behind me came a familiar but unexpected voice. "Mr. Wells?"

Agatha had sneaked out and tracked me down. I'd not seen her coming.

"Hello, Agatha." I smiled at her, then remembering Barco, looked to where he had been to see how he reacted to the presence of this young stranger. To my surprise, he was no longer there. Like a stage conjurer he had vanished, probably going around the other side of the structure, but so quickly it really was like a magician's trick.

"Agatha, good to see you again . . . have you come out to tell me something, or just to say good-bye?"

"I came out to tell you to be careful,

because I remember who the men were that Mr. Flynn talked to about the kidnapping plan. They are Matt and Andrew Kerns . . . two very bad men. My Freeman uncles hate them . . . but my uncles hate most people."

"Including me, Agatha."

"Yes . . . but they are wrong about you. You are a nice man."

"Thank you for saying that. But these Kerns you talked about . . . brothers?"

"Cousins. My uncle Bill says they killed a couple of fellows in another county, and came here to get away from the law. One of them's real young, the other one ten or twelve years older."

"I'll watch out for them. But there's more than just two who were involved, I think."

"Mr. Wells, who was that man you were talking to, the one who went around the other side of the building?"

"Just a man."

"It looked like somebody bad . . . it looked like Tate Barco."

"Really? I'll tell him . . . he'll think that's funny."

She smiled at me, the sweetest smile I'd seen in a long time. I reached out and patted her shoulder and thought how marvelous it would be to one day have a family and children of my own.

She turned and was gone. Then I turned, looking for Barco. He came back around, looking angry.

"Damned little cuss . . . a man like me can't afford to have folks pop up from nowhere to see me and go tell somebody else. She'll run back in there and tell old Flynn that Tate Barco hisself is out in the yard."

"I doubt she will . . . she doesn't much like Flynn."

"She and I see eye to eye, then, even if she is still a runt."

"That little girl has already given us a real hand," I told him. Briefly I described some of what had transpired inside, being careful of my words because this was, after all, Tate Barco I was talking to.

"You ain't married, are you, Wells?"

"No. Sorry to say it, but I'm not."

"Married can be a good thing, a really fine thing, sometimes. And it can be hard other times. Having children is the same way. Sometimes it's fine, other times they break your heart."

"What about Merry?"

"I guess I broke *her* heart, Mr. Wells. It bothers me sometimes, for I know how she thinks of people like me."

"Maybe it isn't too late to fix things with

254

her, Barco. She's a sweet and wonderful girl, from all I can tell. You can make her proud of you by doing the right thing and turning that money over to Flynn. Then you can make amends for your crimes in other ways."

"Like hanging. They've got me labeled for murder, you know."

And rightly so. "Sometimes doing what is right can be costly," I said.

"Easy for you to say. It ain't your neck that would snap in the noose."

"You know, Barco, it generally goes easier on folks who cooperate with the law."

"The law has never gone easy with me . . . the only way I've been able to deal with it is to always keep one step ahead of it. Hey, Jed . . . what did that little girl say about who it is who has Merry?"

"The name Kerns mean anything to you?"

The man looked like he might pass out. His face went white and his lip twitched and trembled. "God," he said, "we've got to get her out. I know them boys. They're bad, I tell you. Bad. They're foul and lustful kinds of men . . . rapists, I hear tell."

"Good Lord, Barco . . . we have to get her away from them, fast."

"We've got to try."

"No. We've got to succeed."

Barco surprised me. A tear formed in one of his eyes and he reached up to dab it away as it rolled down his cheek. "She looks like her mother, you know. Pretty like her mother . . . same eyes, same lips, same hair. Her mother was the prettiest woman I've ever seen."

"Prettier even than Anne Stover?"

"Prettier than her, yes sir."

"She must have been an angel."

"She was . . . and stuck with an old devil like me."

The ride back out toward the abandoned saddle-making facility was uneventful until we got near the spot and came around that same grove of trees where Barco had first surprised me.

Barco swore suddenly as we came around the grove, seizing up stiffly in the saddle, leaning forward and glaring down the slope across the top of his horse's head. I saw what he was looking at: a man running ahead of us, heading for the big building below. The man, who was boyishly young, turned his head slightly and I caught a good look at his profile. And I knew him.

This was the peeper, the vile intruder who'd peered in Merry Gavin's window. Barco saw his face at the same time I did, and cursed again.

"Who is he?" I asked.

"Kerns . . . Andrew Kerns, the younger and worse of the two cousins . . . he's a rounder and rapist. Look at him . . . no more than a maggot shaped like a man, in my estimation. I'm far from a saint, as you know, but to sully women in the way he does is a crime I don't and won't abide, and I'll not suffer such a man to live. Before this affair is done, I vow to kill him, and his worthless cousin as well."

Unable to get from my mind the memory of him at Merry's window, I found nothing to fault in Barco's grim ambition. In fact, I wished just then that I had my rifle in hand. I could drop the man right now, and I don't think there would be any remorse in it other than the fact that such would alert the occupants of the building to our presence. But it was all theoretical: I was still disarmed, Barco holding all the weapons.

Kerns vanished through the saddlery's big, barn-like door. I looked over at Barco and had the odd experience of realizing I no longer hated the man, murderer though he was. It was clear that in his own way he truly loved his daughter and sought her protection. I sought it as well, for her sake but even more so, if I was honest with myself, because I knew how deeply it would hurt Anne Stover for anything bad to happen to her niece. Anne . . . the beautiful, intelligent, gentle Anne . . . a woman I could easily become quite smitten with. Barco had declared his late wife, Anne's sister-in-law, to be even lovelier, but I could not imagine how that could be. Anne and Merry were truly the most beautiful women I had ever known. Surely none could rival them.

"So the money is hidden in the same place where the kidnappers are," I said. "Now, there's an odd and difficult twist!"

"The money is not inside the building," Barco said. "It is hidden outside it. Buried at a certain place only I know."

"Can you get to it and retrieve it without being seen from the building?"

"I think so . . . though that building has more than its share of knotholes and gaps between wall boards. It all depends upon how watchful they are being."

"I don't think Andrew Kerns saw us just now."

"I don't think he did, either."

"Barco, tell me clearly: do you intend to pay Flynn his ransom? Are you going to be man enough, *father* enough, to put aside your pride and do what has to be done to save Merry?"

"The idea of giving back money to that son of a bitch galls the very gut out of me, Jed Wells. I don't like the thought of it at all. But for Merry, I'd do it. I would."

"Then we've got to get that money in hand. Without getting caught. Because if the men in the saddlery get the money directly, it will never go to Flynn, and there's no telling what would become of Merry."

"I'll get it, and I won't get caught."

18

On the southern side of the huge, rambling building was a stone well, or what remained of one. This had provided the drinking water for those who once worked in the saddlery. Water for tanning and other manufacturing-related purposes apparently had been taken from Repentance Creek, the southernmost reaches of which flowed right through the building. The wall had actually been built up a little higher where the creek went under, and according to Barco, there was a huge gap in the floor to allow access to the water. But no one drank from it, he said. Everyone was too conscious of the many outhouses that emptied into the water back up at the town. Thus the well.

Though many of the stones making up the circular well wall had been taken for other uses after the saddle industry closed, most of it was still present. It was under one of the larger ones, right at the base, that Barco had hidden the money, he said. It was inside a watertight metal box and cleverly covered, he said, so that no one would guess the ground around and beneath the stone had been tampered with. But he knew where and how to dig, and could have the money out again in minutes, he swore.

We'd come to trust each other a little more despite ourselves, and he gave me back my pistol and rifle, and assigned me the task of being ready to shoot anyone who might try to stop him. But he would not be seen, he said, if he did well what he had in mind. He would make a huge circle to the south, then come up from that side toward the building, which had few windows on its southern side. On that I had to take his word; the southern side was hidden to me from where I was. The stone under which he would dig was on the well wall's southern face, Barco said. He could crouch down behind that wall and dig with a small camp shovel he always kept with him, and the odds should be good that he could do the entire task without being seen or heard. He would then make the same sweeping circle, but this time in reverse, and rejoin me where I was.

The plan seemed workable, though certainly not foolproof. It could fall apart in a particularly hazardous way should I be forced to shoot at anyone. My presence and general location could easily be ascertained in that case, and it was easy to picture a grim army of mounted human vermin riding out of that big door and up the slope toward me, overwhelming me before I could drop nearly enough of them from their saddles.

So much hinged upon Barco doing a good job of keeping quiet and hidden while he approached and while he worked. I slapped him on the shoulder and voiced strong encouragement, and didn't allow myself to much consider the irony of now working in harmony with the very outlaw I'd sworn to see punished for the murder of poor David Flynn.

The contours of the land were in our favor in regard to Barco reaching the well without being seen. A little ridge of hills skirted around in the same direction he needed to go, so all he had to do was keep them between him and the saddlery as he rode. He left me and set off, and for a long time nothing at all happened. He went out of sight, and I set my eyes on a small gap between the hills just south of the building. Through there, I was sure, he would emerge.

And eventually he did. He rode through

the gap, dismounted, tethered his horse in some brush, and with the little shovel in hand trotted toward the well. Then I mostly lost sight of him as he knelt and began work. Every now and then I saw his head bob up behind the well, or the curve of his shoulders and upper back, but most of him stayed hidden.

I began paying attention to the door of the saddlery instead of to Barco. And to my dismay, I saw movement there. Men were walking about, just inside the doorway, largely shadowed and hard to see, but every now and then one would step into the brighter area nearest the big door. Why were they there? Had someone seen Barco?

The men were armed with rifles and spent a lot of time scanning the landscape. I ducked low in the little hollow place that hid me, making sure they could not pick me out among the stones and stumps.

Then one of them emerged, the same one we'd watched walk down the hill when we first got here. He looked around as if suspicious something was afoot, then turned sharply as if startled.

He'd turned toward the south, and began edging that way, along the eastern-facing wall of the building. Barco, I figured, had made a noise. In moments he would be discovered. I raised my rifle and took aim at the creeping fellow who was now nearing the corner of the building, around which he would look and surely spot Barco.

It was a long shot, and I was still without my scope, but I thought I could do it. I hesitated, though. Shooting the man would reveal our presence just as quickly as anything Barco might do. And it would reveal *my* presence and location even faster.

The calculating, self-preserving side of me said not to shoot, to let Barco take his own chances. If he was caught, perhaps he would not make mention of me. I could get away from here. Then I would return to Flynn, find out how much money would be required to fulfill the ransom, and obtain it from Clelland, Gage, myself, and any others willing to throw some money in.

My moral side chided me. I was counting on an outlaw to be more virtuous than myself, counting on Barco to take his punishment alone and leave me out of it. Strange as it was, he was my partner now, at least in the effort to bring Merry back safely home, and I owed it to him to take the same chances he did.

I leveled and steadied my rifle, and drew a careful bead on Andrew Kerns, who was now at the corner of the building and looking around toward the well. But I realized that from his angle, Barco was hidden. If Barco would only remain quiet and still a few minutes, this crisis might pass without his presence ever being detected.

Concentrating so hard, I hardly breathed myself. So it was easy to hear the sound of hoof falls in the woodland grove beside and behind me. I turned my head and saw a rider coming slowly through, taking a narrow path, probably made by cattle at some past time, that sliced through the grove, one side to the other. Dear God, I'd been caught! The outlaws below had already sent up someone to get me!

I rolled from my belly onto my back and pulled the rifle around, aiming it at the rider. He moved in a way that told me he was startled, and I knew then that he hadn't been sent after me at all. He hadn't even realized I was here.

The rider halted, became a statue there at the edge of the grove. I frowned, looking deeply at him but not being able to see his face well because of the shadow of his broad hat brim. He slowly reached up and tilted back his hat, letting light spill across his face.

I drew in a deep breath of relief and said, "Charlie Crowder, tether that horse back in the trees there and get over here . . . we've got a situation in progress down below."

A couple of minutes later, I was back on my belly, aiming down the slope again, while Charlie lay on his belly to my right side, squinting and taking it all in.

He'd already told me what had brought him there. The sheriff's posse had made no headway at all and had eventually broken up, but Charlie had realized that the old saddle factory building might be a good place for kidnappers to hide, and had decided to come investigate it on his own. He'd hardly anticipated coming through the grove to find me lying on the ground, aiming my rifle at his face.

"Jed," he asked, "who is that down behind the well?"

"Tate Barco."

"The hell you say!"

"No, it is him, honest truth. He's down there right now digging out the money that we last saw being taken from David Flynn's carpetbag during the stagecoach robbery. He's going to use it to pay the ransom for Merry."

"Then for God's sake, why are you acting like you're about to shoot him?"

"Not him, Charlie, but those others at the door. Those are the kidnappers, and I'm

266

afraid the one over at the corner will see Barco behind the well. So far he hasn't, and Barco has been keeping still so that he won't. I think Barco knows that they are there, otherwise he'd still be digging and prying at the rock of the well wall."

"So who is behind the kidnapping?"

"Take a guess."

"Albert Flynn."

"Precisely."

"You know it for a fact?"

"He's the one waiting for ransom, so that makes him guilty in my book. But he officially denies any involvement, while simultaneously assuring that Merry will be safe if he gets back the money stolen from Repentance Creek Bank."

"Son of a bitch!"

"Ain't he, though?"

"Are you sure Merry is down there?"

"I haven't seen her, but I know that's where the kidnappers are hiding out, and I have reason to feel sure she is there."

"We should go down and get her, then."

"Too many of them, Charlie. We don't have the advantage."

"When I'm mad, I count for as good as five men, Jed. You're probably the same."

"No, I'm good for three, maybe four at best. But the trouble is, even if we were both

equal to an army, it still takes only two bullets to eliminate us."

"Or one, if I was in front of you and it
went through me and into you."

"You're bantering, I know, but I've seen
that happen. Back during the war, I caused
it to happen. More than one target with a
single shot is an achievement of honor for a
sharpshooter, Charlie."

"Take a look, Jed."

I did, and was relieved to see that Andrew
Kern had moved back to join the others.
From his easy manner and way of move-
ment, it was obvious he had not detected
Barco's presence after all. Thank God!

"So you and Barco are working together
now, are you?"

"Only to the extent we both want Merry
safe and free. He's working hard and smart
to see that happens, so yes, I'm working
with him."

"Jed, I want to get a look inside that place
down there."

"How? They're six men at the door right
now. You so much as stand up and they'll
see you."

"What about the far side? Another door?
I'd think there would be."

"Probably . . . but it might be guarded,
too. And we can't do anything until Barco

is in the clear."

"You think he'd really give all that money back to Flynn?"

"I do."

"I'll believe it when I see it."

"Know what I have trouble believing, Charlie?"

"What's that?"

"That Tate Barco has gotten away with his crimes as long as he has. You'd think that such a law legend as Strickland would have found a way to get him by now, even if some of the population does give aid and hiding to Barco at times."

"Having just finished riding with the sheriff's posse, Jed, I can tell you that Strickland is a good man, a man who truly is a legend, and who was among the greatest of the Rangers, but he's now a man growing old and slow. This county needs a better sheriff than he can ever be."

"Would Harrison East be able to handle the job?"

"Not well. He's fine for town marshal in a little place like Repentance Creek, but the county would be too much for him, in my opinion."

"You should run for sheriff yourself, Charlie."

"Nah. Not me. You should take up residence here and do it instead, Jed.".

"Yeah . . . I'm sure local folks would elect me without a second thought. You can't be serious, Charlie. I'm a newcomer, and one with very little experience at that. And no ambitions toward law enforcement."

"You're also the local hero . . . keep that in mind."

"You're actually serious, I think."

"I'm telling you, Jed, you could do the job, and people here would elect you. Once more of them come to understand that Strickland can't handle the work anymore."

All this talk had distracted me, and when I looked down the slope again, Barco was no longer at the well, but running across open ground toward the place he'd hidden his horse. He had a small metal box in hand.

"Come on, Jed," said Charlie. "Let's go down there and meeting him coming back. Then we can turn back and circle in a little farther than he did, and come out on the west side of the building. I feel sure there's a door, and maybe we'll be able to actually see Merry, and get her out."

"Hold up, Charlie. I'm not shifting the original plan at this point. Barco and I worked out what to do, and we'll do it that way. He's got the money, so we can go pay the ransom, and then we'll haul Flynn's rump out here and make him order her freedom with his own lips."

"I don't think he'll do it."

"Why not?"

"Pride. He'll never let Barco get one up on him."

I'd heard something like that before, from Barco himself. I wasn't glad to hear it again.

19

In times to come after that hour there on the hillside, looking across a rifle sight at the big building where saddlemakers once plied their trade, I would have many occasions to experience the stubbornness of Charlie Crowder. But this was my first real exposure to it, and it got me into something of an uproar.

"Jed, we can't just lay here and hope that Barco comes back," he said. "Guarantee you, that scoundrel will change his thinking now he's got his money in hand again. He'll leave poor Merry where she is and take off to Mexico or someplace and say to hell with it all. We ought to ride around to meet him if for no other cause than to see that he don't do that."

I still didn't like the idea of changing horses in midstream, as it were, but Charlie's idea wasn't all that much of a stretch. All it meant was that Barco and I would meet up again a little quicker than if I waited for him to come all the way back here. Charlie pressed, and I yielded.

We got our horses from the woods and rode out of the far side of the grove so as not to be visible from the building, then followed Barco's route around the base of the hiding hills. We made fast time, and it was pleasant to be fully out of potential view of the kidnappers.

But I worried that Charlie might be right about Barco, and that he might already have absconded with the money in some different direction. The next minutes would tell the story. If he was keeping his end of the deal, we would ride into one another's view at any moment.

I'd given up hope when suddenly he appeared. Barco's horse came loping into view, the outlaw astride his saddle and grinning broadly — until he saw I was not alone. He slowed nearly to a stop and rode his horse in behind a tree.

"Don't worry!" I called as loudly as I dared. "It's all right, Barco! It's just Charlie Crowder, and he's with us on this!"

Barco eventually emerged, looking quite worried, his dark eyes studying Charlie as if Charlie might suddenly turn into a bomb and blow us all up.

"Where the hell did he come from?" Barco asked.

"Howdy, dear friend Barco," Charlie said. "I'm mighty glad to see you faring so well, too."

I glared at Charlie. Now was not the time to get Barco angry. "Charlie was with the sheriff's posse, which has broken up, and it came to his mind that the saddlery needed to be looked at as a possible hiding place for the kidnappers."

"Smart man," said Barco.

"My old mother thinks so, anyway," Charlie replied.

"You got the money, I see," I said, looking at the dirty metal box that now stuck out the top of one saddlebag.

"Told you I would, didn't I? Didn't get caught, neither."

"You almost did," said Charlie. "Tell me something, Barco: ain't there a door on the west side of that building?"

"Yes. . . . Not as large as the east door, but there is one."

"I want to see it."

"Why?"

"Maybe we can see Merry . . . get her out without you having to put that money back in Flynn's hands."

Barco's look evidenced that he liked that

274

particular idea. I had to admit that I did, too. Even though Flynn had truly been victimized when his bank was robbed, and the money rightly should be returned to him regardless of his personal morals and disposition, it was impossible to like the idea of him coming out to the good after commissioning such an evil act as the kidnapping of an innocent young woman.

Charlie's idea won the day. Barco was familiar with the building, so he led the way. We hid our horses, checked our rifles and handguns, and headed back the way Barco had just come. We passed the gap through the hills, and went further on so we could reach that hidden side of the building.

And all at once, we were there. The line of hills petered away to a mere line of boulders, and then nothing. Across the top of the boulders we saw the building, and another door that was a narrower version of the huge one on the other side. "There it is," Barco said. "Can't see much for the shadows, though."

He was right. It was even harder to see on this side than on the other. But I had an impression of someone inside there, moving . . . or maybe it was merely a stray dog.

"What now?" Charlie asked. "We can't very well just walk in there."

I opened my mouth to voice some kind of answer, though in reality I had none, and before I could speak, we heard the scream.

Loud, piercing, feminine . . . the voice of Merry Gavin. It made my knees turn to water. Struck dumb, I gaped at Charlie, then at Barco . . . and was for some reason surprised to see the depth of emotion revealed on the latter's face. He'd gone white, sickly looking, like at any moment he might heave up his last meal. "Oh, God!" he whispered. "What are they doing to her?"

She screamed again . . . this was not merely fear, but suffering. Charlie and I looked at each other again in a wordless communication, then vaulted over the boulders before us and ran at full tilt toward the door. Charlie took one side, I the other. We looked at each other and Charlie counted: "One . . . two . . ."

Together we shouted "Three!" and pivoted into the open doorway, rifles out and ready to shoot. No one shot at us, but there was a jumble of distressed male voices from somewhere inside, just muffled enough to let us know that they were in one of the framed-in central rooms. Then Merry screamed again, louder than ever, and her voice cut off with the sound of a loud, hard slap of palm against flesh. What followed this time was more of a moan than a scream.

It infuriated me beyond words. I lunged farther back into the building, deeper into the darkness, Charlie mirroring my moves beside me. We reached a closed door and found it locked. Another shared glance and silent communication, and we kicked it in together, Charlie with his right foot, I with my left. The wood splintered and the entire door burst off its hinges and shivered to the dirt floor.

We saw another dark room, another doorway, but this one was open, and beyond it was a pool of lamplight. We'd found where they were — a lighted room that otherwise would have been nearly as black as a cavern, for there were no openings to the outside other than the knotholes and cracks of the wall. A man appeared in the doorway, and I was startled and sickened to see that he was fumbling with his trousers, as if we'd interrupted him in the act of taking them off or putting them on. He staggered back when he saw us, and reached under his vest. He brought out a small pistol, lifted it . . .

Charlie and I fired in tandem and the bullets both hit him in mid-chest. I saw a red spray fan out behind him as his body kicked back and fell hard onto the floor. Merry screamed again, and this time it was quite loud because she, too, obviously was in the same room as the man we'd just shot.

Someone behind us . . . we wheeled and recognized Barco in time to stop ourselves from shooting him, too. He advanced to us, face still pallid, legs trembling so badly he could hardly walk straight. He looked things over, seemingly comprehended what had gone on here, and with his pistol in hand marched boldly through the door, as fearless as if he had just danced the Ghost Dance and was invulnerable to harm. He froze inside the door and let out a loud gasp and a string of furious profanities, followed up by a roar of the purest anger I'd ever encountered. Then he lunged forward and I could no longer see him.

Apparently stirred by Barco's boldness, Charlie also passed through the doorway, and also yelled in seeming anger. I followed, and I did not shout, for what I saw made me lose my breath.

Merry was there, tied with her back to a support post, a rope around her wrists, another around her stomach, and a third around her neck, pulling her head back tightly against the post. She was wearing the same dress that she'd worn at her aunt's party, which was so recent but now seemed a year back. But the dress was torn, barely hanging on her, leaving her humiliatingly exposed.

Before her was a man, wearing only long underwear, his outer clothing lying in heaps here and there about the room. He gazed at we three intruders with his mouth hanging open stupidly, then settled his stare on Barco. "I know you!" he said. "You're Tate Barco! I rode with you once, remember? The time we robbed the freight office over in Merritt?"

"What are you doing to her?" Barco demanded. "Is this what it appears to be?"

The man grinned weakly, forcing out a chuckle, as if he could defuse this situation in such a way. Barco roared again, raised his pistol, and shot the man three times in the chest. He was dead before he hit the floor.

"I've got no use for a man who would rape a woman," Barco said.

Merry Gavin wailed like a lost soul, her face distorted and tear-streaked. Barco went to her and began pulling what remained of her dress back onto her, restoring her modesty. He did it with the gentle manner of a father with his child, and at that moment I saw the man as much more a normal human being than I had to this point. He began to weep, a man hurt because his daughter was hurt, and he leaned forward and talked softly to her, asking her things I could not hear. She replied just as softly, calling him "Mr. Barco," and I think that hurt him, because his tears came faster. "I am your father," he said. "I am your father, Merry."

We heard noise outside, behind us, and realized that the others in the building had heard the shots and responded not by coming to us through the building itself, but going out and circling around it to come in the secondary entrance we'd just used. Charlie and I headed back to that entrance just as the first of the newcomers appeared, levering a rifle. I shot quickly and he never had a chance to fire off that bullet. He fell, and another man, running in, tripped over his body. The man tried to get up fast, drawing a pistol, and Charlie made quick work of him by pounding the butt of his rifle onto the back of the man's head, with skull-shattering force. The man died with a final groan.

Charlie flipped his rifle, levered it, and jerked backward as a bullet from outside clipped the fleshy outer portion of his left arm. Some of the blood, along with some tiny fragments of Charlie's muscle, slapped me across the chest and chin. Charlie quickly fired back, and given his triumphant yell right after, apparently found his target. But he was still exposed, so he moved back and to the side, making himself invisible from outside the building.

A man came through the door, raising a shotgun. I shot him dead and he fell atop the man Charlie had clubbed. The dead men actually helped us out, for they made it impossible for anyone to enter the door quickly. It was necessary to clamber across the dead to gain entrance. One man tried it, and Charlie fired and made him the top corpse in the stack.

Gunfire inside — Barco shooting at someone. So apparently some of the band had indeed come back through the bowels of the building itself, the group having divided itself by chance or design. When it appeared that no one else was going to appear at the doorway, I reentered the room where Merry was captive, and saw that Barco had freed her. With ropes dragging after her, she was scrambling to a corner, taking what little refuge she could there. She was the most pitiable sight I'd ever seen, crying violently, terrified beyond expression.

I hated the men who had done this to her . . . hated Flynn for sponsoring it, hated the men who had carried it out. I wondered how much she had endured, and prayed that we had arrived in time to deter any actual violation of her person. I dared to think that we had, given the partially clothed condition in which we'd found both victim and attacker.

Andrew Kerns appeared in the doorway of the room. I'd lost track of him in the hub-bub. Merry looked up, blanched, and screamed as if burned when she saw him. This was the one in particular who Barco had said was a known rapist, and Merry's violent reaction to his presence lessened my hope that she had somehow gone unmo-lested during her captivity so far.

I put myself between him and her, not even able to abide the thought of his eyes on her, and he glared at me hatefully. Sud-denly he came at me, something flashing in his hand, and I felt a sharp stabbing pain in my lower left side, followed by a hot flow of blood. He pulled back his hand, a bloodied shiv in his grip. I'd just been stabbed.

"It's not wise to stab a man with a gun," I said, and shot him just to prove the point. Merry screamed at the noise of the shot, then began a low, rising laugh when she saw him fall. The bullet had hit him in the sternum and gone in at a heart-finding angle. He died with a look of terror on his face, as if he'd been allowed a quick advance look into the hell that surely awaited him.

I went to Merry, knelt beside her, and spoke words of comfort, removing the remnants of her bonds. Crying in a different way now, the kind of crying that lets out tension and fear, she put her arms around my neck and hugged me.

"God bless you, girl," I said. "And God protect you from wicked men from now on."

"Come on," said Tate Barco. "Time for us to go."

"Where?" I asked him.

"We take Merry home, give her to her aunt for love and comfort, for she surely wants none from the beast that is her father."

Merry regained control of her emotions enough to speak.

"You are no beast, Mr. Barco," she said. "You have rescued me today at great risk to yourself, and shown me signs that there is in you, after all, some love for your own offspring. I never believed it before. But forgive me if I cannot call you my father. My father, to me, is John Gavin, who raised me. Can you understand that, Mr. Barco?"

"Yes, I can. And I don't fault your feelings. But just once, just so I can hear it, will you do me the favor of calling me Papa?

Just once?"

She looked at him, the man who had left her to the care of others in childhood and murdered her fiancé in adulthood, and from somewhere within drew up a reserve of will and strength. She managed to smile, and said, "I think I can do that . . . Papa."

Barco's tears came harder than ever.

"But listen to me," she said to him, rising and going to his side. "I must now ask you a favor. You know, as do all of us, that you have spent your life bringing bad things into the world. I now ask you, as your daughter. . . . I ask you, Papa, to do me the honor of reversing that course and bringing good to the world instead. I want you to turn away from the life you've led and become an honest man of honest labor. In doing that you can bring good to the world by taking away one thing that has been bad — the man you've been before. You can take him away, and make the world a better place for it. Do you understand, Papa?"

He nodded, hugging her. "I understand . . . and there is more that I can do even than that."

"Then do it, Papa. Do it for me."

He looked at me. "You coming with me, Wells?"

"Coming where?"

284

"We've got ransom to deliver, remember?"

"I don't understand," I told Barco as I rode along beside him in the direction of Repentance Creek and the home of Albert Flynn. "Why give the ransom to Flynn now? We've already gained Merry's safety. Does he deserve to be paid for what he did to her?"

"You heard what Merry said to me," Barco said. "I've got to change my ways. Got to repent, like folks did along this creek back when this was a camp meeting ground. Well, to repent you got to change, and you got to give back what you've took that wasn't yours to have."

"I think something's changed inside you, Barco."

"I hope so. I guess I've been doing some deep thinking."

"And what have you concluded?" I asked.

"That in the end, we're all going to get what we deserve, and I'd like to do some things with my life that make me deserve something other than retribution and evil. Because so far, the only good thing I've given this world is that pretty young woman we just saved. And I'm honored by God above that he let me bring something so good into being."

"Amen, Tate Barco," said Charlie

Crowder, riding on Barco's other side.

We rode through the very center of town, Barco making no attempt to hide his face or otherwise avoid being identified. Of course our little three-man parade generated a lot of attention — the two town "heroes" who faced off against Barco in the stage robbery now riding at his side like old friends. No doubt it was an odd sight.

We'd left Merry at Anne Stover's, and ridden away with the two of them talking intently. Merry would tell Anne more about what had happened to her than she would ever tell to a man such as me or Charlie. I prayed that there was little to tell, and that Merry would somehow shake off the scars of an ordeal she never should have suffered.

"I have to ask you again, Barco," I said, "in that we're talking about people getting what they deserve, does Albert Flynn deserve to have that money put back in his hands? He's the reason Merry went through what she did."

"I know, I know," he replied. "Don't worry . . . he will get exactly what he has earned. I intend to see to that. I'm about to do what Merry asked me to do."

"She wanted you to give the money to Flynn?" asked Charlie.

"She did . . . because that's what her lover

wanted to be done at the time he died. He was on his way to give it back to his pap, and me and Hiram robbed the stage and stopped that from happening. Now it falls to me to fix that."

"I do believe you're a changing man, Tate," I told him. "It's inspiring to see." I paused. "But there are yet murders on your record, and I and Charlie remain sworn deputies of the county sheriff. We can't let you walk away, no matter what."

"I know. You won't have to."

"You're ready to pay the price?"

"I'm ready to become a good man, and do what is right, just like Merry asked me to."

I could hardly believe my ears.

We reached Flynn's house. "You know he doesn't want you to deliver the money," I told him. "He told me to bring it to him."

"Fine," said Barco, handing me the box. "You do it. But I'll follow you in. After what that man had done to my girl, he's going to face me, whether he likes it or not."

"I can't fault *that* notion," Charlie said.

We rode into the yard and were greeted there by young Agatha, who came out of a smokehouse bearing a small ham, no doubt fulfilling an errand for her mother. She gaped when she saw Tate Barco, and her face became so white that her freckles stood out in stark accent. Turning, she ran inside.

"Tate, he might shoot you if you walk in that door," I said.

"If he does, he does."

"Are you sure you're thinking straight in all this?" asked Charlie.

"For the first time in my life I'm thinking straight," Barco replied.

We tied our horses to the porch rail and walked onto the porch together. I knocked on the door and Agatha's mother answered. She looked as scared as her daughter when she saw it really was Barco who'd come calling.

"I've got something Mr. Flynn will want to have," I said, holding up the little box. She hardly glanced at it, unable to quit staring at Barco. "Is he here, or at the bank?"

"Usually he would be at the bank, but today he came home early, not feeling well."

"Aw, is the poor fellow feeling puny?" Barco asked in a sarcasm-permeated voice. "Let's go in and wish him well."

She stood back and let us enter, then told us to remain in the front hall. She went to a heavy, gleaming mahogany door off the west end of the front parlor, knocked and entered. Flynn's personal study or office, I supposed.

I was right. A few moments later the door opened, and Flynn himself stepped out, expression reflecting skepticism that gave way to staggering belief when he saw that, yes indeed, Tate Barco himself was in his front hallway. Flynn gaped at the outlaw, who glared back at him.

I stepped forward. "I have something for you," I said, holding up the box. "Here is the money that was taken from the Repentance Creek Bank. Most of it, anyway. Some was spent, but most is here."

"Barco!" Flynn said in a raspy whisper. "How dare you come into my home! How dare you set your foul foot on my floor!"

"How dare you have my daughter captured and misused by a gang of vermin?" Barco replied, and I thought it a powerful answer.

"I had nothing to do with that," Flynn said, the lie hanging in the air like a bad stench.

"She's safe now," Barco said. "We were able to rescue her. But we brought you your money, anyway, because your son was bringing it back to you when he was killed, and it seemed right to fulfill what he wasn't able to finish."

"Since when have you cared what is right, you bastard?" Flynn asked, stepping forward and taking the box from my hand.

"Since I had a good talk with my own little girl, mostly," replied Barco. "She asked me to change my ways, to bring good things to the world and rid the world of bad things, too. So I've come to do that. I've brought you the money and fulfilled what your son wanted done, so I've brought a good thing in doing that. Now, it's time to rid the world of two bad things. I'm going to do it right now."

With that, Barco drew his pistol, lifted it, and aimed it at Flynn's face. Flynn stumbled backward, into his study, and closed the door. Barco fired three quick shots through the wood and we heard Flynn's body thump on the floor on the other side of the door.

"One bad thing gone," Barco said.

Charlie went to the door and pushed it open, having to scoot Flynn's body to do so. He entered the study and Barco and I followed.

Flynn was on the floor, chest punctured three times by bullets, his mouth open and wet, his eyes staring straight up and beginning to lose their light. There were white circles around them, and across his nose — the "death mask" was on him, marking him as a doomed man.

"Murderer!" he whispered up at Barco, who had knelt beside him. "Murderer!"

I was amazed he could even find the voice. Barco actually grinned back down at him, and said, "I *am* a murderer, a bad man. And I admit it and confess it right here. I murdered your son and I murdered them stage coach fellows, and I've murdered others I need not mention. I'm like you, Flynn . . . a vile and evil thing, a bad thing. And now it's time for me to take one more bad thing out of this world, like I've took you out."

Barco opened his mouth, thrust in his pistol, and fired. He flopped over backward, the back of his head blasted off much like David Flynn's had been that grim day at the stagecoach.

Flynn made an odd noise in his throat, tried to lift his head and see Barco's body. He managed it, then died in the midst of the effort, his skull thunking against the hardwood floor as his head fell limply back.

"Have you ever seen the like?" Charlie said.

"No," I replied. "I have not."

20

One year later

Charlie looked fine in his new suit, and the badge gleaming on his lapel only added to his dignity and excellent appearance. He stood with a stiff smile on his lean face and didn't even blink as the flash powder went off and his image etched itself onto the plate inside the boxy, tall camera.

"That it for me?" he asked.

"That's it," I replied, shaking his hand. "And I can't thank you enough, Charlie. I can't think of a man I'd rather have stand up for me on a day this special. You've made this a wedding to remember."

"Dang, Jed, do you have to rub salt in the wound?" he said. "This was supposed to be *my* day, remember?" He turned to my lovely new bride and said, "Anne, how could you have made such a poor choice when you had such a fine one available to you?"

"You never asked me, Charlie, remember?"

"Well, I never did, did I!"

"No . . . but I have to tell you, I'd have had to turn you down. You're just too much man for me . . . you rugged cattleman types are overwhelming to a woman who spends her life surrounded by the gentle world of books."

"Why, hell — pardon me for the French — I read, too! I'm halfway through Jed's newest book."

And new it was, literally just off the press. I'd not finished scanning through my own copy yet . . . Charlie was actually farther along than I was, but then, it's always harder to read one's own work.

"It's a much better book than it would have been if not for my wise intervention," said Walter Gage, behind Charlie.

Charlie turned. "How's that?"

"Jed had a lame-brained notion of writing a story based on a character in his prior book. I'm the one who steered him onto the real story that fate had handed him. And I think you'll agree the choice was a wise one."

"Well, I ain't been able to put it down at night since I started it," Charlie said. "I particularly like that handsome cowboy fellow in the story. I think he'll wind up marrying the pretty librarian in the end."

"Sometimes life imitates art, and other times it sets its own course," I said. "Charlie, thanks again for being my best man. And Walter, thank you for everything — too many things to name."

"Bah! I'm just an old fool who thinks he can do anything, and tries."

"And succeeds," said Anne, my wife, as she leaned forward to kiss the old man.

"Hey, I'm the one who you said your 'I dos' to," I said.

"Only because I'm a little young for Walter," she said. "If that wasn't the case, I'd have already married him years ago."

"I'm painfully aware of that," I told her. "But since it's Walter we're talking about, I'll forgive you . . . and maybe even him."

"Speaking of age difference, how much do you think that really matters?" Charlie asked.

"I don't think it matters much at all," Anne replied. "You have my blessing, Charlie. I'd love to call you my son-in-law, even if you are older than I am."

"Well, we'll see if we can't make that happen . . . but I'll have to persuade Merry to hitch up with an old cattleman like me to do it, and she may not favor the notion."

"I have reason to think otherwise," Anne said. "Just keep at it, Sheriff Crowder. You'll succeed at catching yourself a good wife just as you did at getting yourself elected to office."

"I like this sheriffing trade," Charlie said. "My only problem is my deputy who wants to spend all his time writing instead of tending to the law."

"I'm only a part-time deputy, Charlie," I reminded him.

"So you are. Well, folks, got to go. You two enjoy your wedding trip, and be sure to name your first boy after me."

"It's a bargain," I said.

He turned and walked away, Merry coming around the side of the church and taking his arm. They walked off together.

I turned to Anne and kissed her on the lips. "And to think I was ready to leave Texas when I'd hardly gotten here!"

"I'm glad you didn't."

"So am I, Mrs. Wells. So am I."

"I have reason to think otherwise," Anne said, "Just keep at it," Sheriff Crowder. You'll succeed at catching yourself a good wife just as you did at getting yourself elected to office.

"I like this sheriffing trade," Charlie said. "My only problem is my deputy who wants to spend all his time writing instead of reading to the law."

"I'm only a part-time deputy, Charlie," I reminded him.

"So you are. Well, folks, got to go. You two enjoy your wedding trip, and be sure to name your first boy after me."

"It's a bargain," I said.

He turned and walked away, Merry coming around the side of the church and taking my arm. They walked off together.

I turned to Anne and kissed her on the lips. "And to think I was ready to leave Texas when I'd hardly gotten here."

"I'm glad you didn't."

"So am I, Mrs. Wells. So am I."

ABOUT THE AUTHOR

Tobias Cole is a pseudonym for a well-known author of Western fiction. He lives in Tennessee.

The employees of Thorndike Press hope you have enjoyed this Large Print book. All our Thorndike, Wheeler, and Kennebec Large Print titles are designed for easy reading, and all our books are made to last. Other Thorndike Press Large Print books are available at your library, through selected bookstores, or directly from us.

For information about titles, please call:
(800) 223-1244

or visit our website at:
gale.com/thorndike

To share your comments, please write:
Publisher
Thorndike Press
10 Water St., Suite 310
Waterville, ME 04901